The Bist
Sacrifice I

The

Demon

Shadow

Timothy Patrick Means

Mad Dog Press

The Demon Shadow
Book One of The Bishops' Sacrifice Series
Copyright 2021 by Timothy Patrick Means

ISBN: 978-1-7376017-0-8
Printed in the United States of America

Published by
Mad Dog Publications
Boise, Idaho

sacrificetheinnocentsbooks.com

Cover design by Eric Labacz, www.labaczdesign.com

I dedicate this book to my loving wife, Janice, and our new additions to the family, Spencer and Avery Means. You have willingly come into our lives with hearts full of love and devotion to teach us the need for patience.

Chapter 1

Barbara Bishop Harding finished dressing and closed her armoire. Staring at herself in the mirrored door, she could see the punishing effects of stress that left her looking haggard and old before her time. Disgusted with her appearance, she went into the bathroom and grabbed the hairbrush, noticing the bristles of the comb were collecting long strands of hair at an alarming rate. Nothing could prevent the anxiety, nor the fear, she had felt since her daughter had gone missing—and as a result, her body was paying the price for her stressful existence.

As she began her morning chores by stripping their bed, she accidentally knocked off the small picture from the nightstand. Picking it up off the floor and staring at the happy faces, profound sorrow pierced her soul. The photo had been taken while the family was on vacation: Her two daughters were playing tag with their father, Mark, in a field of colorful daisies on a summer day not long ago.

The portrait had been on her nightstand since before Melissa had gone missing, but today it somehow left her feeling empty—her world could no longer be ordinary again.

It ripped at her heart; her grief so heavy she thought it might destroy her. She couldn't stare at the photo any longer so she slipped it inside her nightstand drawer and closed it tightly.

As she looked out her bedroom window at the cold, slate-gray sky, she felt alone in the world. The weight of Melissa's disappearance was more than she could bear, and unstoppable tears slowly trickled down her cheeks.

The more she thought about Melissa, the more a mournful knife twisted in her soul. At long last her tears were spent; she felt more tired than she had at any time in her life. She knew this feeling would only end when her sixteen-year-old daughter was back home, alive and well.

Emotionally drained, she returned to the bathroom. Pulling out several facial tissues from the decorative box, she dabbed the sobbing tears from her blue eyes. She glanced in the mirror, disgusted at her reflection. There, looking back, was someone exhausted and worn out.

Thankfully, she didn't have to go anywhere that day. She had been given a few weeks off from work, but instead of helping her cope with the loss, it caused her to reflect more on her missing daughter, especially in the still quiet morning hours when Mark was away at work and her twelve-year-old daughter, Rachel, was at school.

Noticing the time on the alarm clock, she decided to eat breakfast, even if she wasn't hungry. She felt no joy in anything she did. Life was just a series of events she had to work at achieving. Images of Melissa constantly played in her mind, leaving little room for anything else. Nothing could heal the deep hurt. Each dark day felt like a lifetime, with no end in sight.

Heading back to the bathroom after her quick breakfast, she spent a short time applying her makeup. Content with her appearance, she walked back to the kitchen. Dumping her cold coffee in the sink, she rinsed out the cup and set it on the counter to be washed.

She heard the screech of tires out front and, glancing out her kitchen window, saw a familiar car pull into their driveway. Before the vehicle came to a complete stop, Susan Bernstein shot out of the passenger seat, calling her name. Barbara ran to the front door where Susan was already waiting impatiently. The look on her face said it all.

Barbara collapsed in Susan's arms and began to cry.

Holding the inconsolable mother tightly, Susan whispered, "We rushed home as soon as we got the ship-to-shore telegram telling of Melissa's disappearance. Tell us what happened!"

"Please, I want you both to know I hesitated to contact you. I knew that telling you about Melissa's disappearance would cause you both to cancel your vacation plans and rush home. But I had no one else to turn to; you're her godparents so I knew you would hate me if I didn't tell you."

"You were right in sending that telegram; now we're home. Please tell us everything."

Susan put an arm around Barbara's shoulders as they walked inside, her husband, John hurriedly, following behind, silently giving his support.

Barbara held onto her friend tightly as she tried to explain the essential details of Melissa's disappearance. Susan was nearly twenty years her senior, a motherly figure, and a close friend.

Barbara had lost her mother at an early age, and in a family with two brothers and her father, she had often felt the lack of a woman's presence. When she met her, Susan had filled in the gaps in her emotional life, her longing for a mother's understanding.

She had met Susan as an intern at an investment brokerage firm. Instantly, they became close friends. Susan's husband, John, was retired from the U.S. Marshal's Service. Barbara's father had passed away from cancer a few years before, her elder brother, Spencer, had been killed in a motorcycle accident, and Butch, the younger brother, was in prison for armed robbery. Now the Bernsteins were the closest thing to a family she had. To see them now eased some of the heavy burdens from her shoulders.

"We caught the very next flight available as soon as our cruise ship docked in port. It wasn't easy, but we managed to get home as quickly as we could," Susan announced.

John stood by listening, without making any remarks. As a display of stability, he wrapped his large frame around Barbara and hugged her warmly.

"Tell us what you know so far," he asked.

Taking the tissue that Susan offered, she wiped away the tears and described the events of the previous Tuesday afternoon.

"It was just a few days after you and Susan left on your cruise when Melissa disappeared."

Regaining her composure, she recalled events of that fateful day, leaving out none of the details.

"That afternoon Rachel called me at work; it was a little past four, and Melissa hadn't gotten home from school. You know that's not like her. Rachel went to our neighbor Mrs. Andersen to use the phone to tell me where she was. She was upset because she couldn't get into the house."

Barbara paused, lost in thought as she stared into space, reliving the events of that day in her mind. It was as if the nightmare had returned.

"Barbara," Susan called out, "are you still with us?"

"Forgive me," she whispered. "It all seems like yesterday. Where was I? Oh yes, Rachel called me from the neighbor's house to ask if it was all right if she stayed there until her sister got home. It was cold that day, and I quickly agreed. I was furious at Melissa because of it, but what could I do?"

Susan reassuringly answered, "In that situation, not much."

"Of course, I realized what an inconvenience it might be for my neighbor. I was grateful that Mrs. Anderson was kind enough to allow Rachel to stay at all.

"When I got home, I was sure Melissa would be there. But the lights weren't on. As soon as I opened the car door, Rachel came running frantically from the neighbor's house, shouting that her sister still hadn't gotten home from school."

Barbara dabbed the tears from her eyes and continued. "I felt like my heart had stopped. The first thing I did was call the school to ask if the bus had broken down. But all the buses had already returned to the station, with no children left behind. I called Melissa's friends—none of them had seen her. It was around six o'clock when Mark got home from work. As soon as he stepped into the house, he could tell something was wrong.

"I explained that Melissa still wasn't home from school, and Mark began asking what I had done to find her. I told him I'd called the school and checked with her friends. Mark got in his car and frantically drove throughout the neighborhood. He stopped by her best friend Stacy's house. She told him she hadn't seen Melissa since the fifth period.

"When Mark got back home, we went to the school grounds and searched for any sign of her, but we found nothing. That evening we explored the entire city.

"Finally, we called the police to report Melissa's disappearance. A police sergeant named Hargrove monitored the search. He told us a runaway child—a teenager—leaves home voluntarily, but we knew in our hearts Melissa would never run away; she had no reason.

"Mark was desperate. He got into his car again and drove around the city, searching for places Melissa could be, but he returned with no results. The following day he began making phone calls and enlisted some of his friends to help in the search. They explored the streets and neighborhoods for days afterward and came up empty.

The result was the same: Melissa was gone, except now the police started asking us all kinds of personal questions about our family and marriage."

"Barbara, it's just routine questioning," John put in.

"Asking if our marriage was a happy one and if we beat our children or if we did drugs, and if we had ever molested our daughters," Barbara snapped.

Grabbing Barbara's arm, Susan tried to comfort her but to no avail.

"Mark was upset," Barbara continued, "and began shouting at the police investigator, a Lieutenant Reed. I felt miserable. Soon afterward the police set up surveillance at our home and waited for a phone call from a kidnapper—it never came. They did find one thing—a piece of Melissa's torn sweater, with some grease and small amounts of blood, near an abandoned house not far from the school grounds.

"A suspicious dark-colored utility van was spotted driving in the neighborhood, but none was ever found matching that description. It's been a week now. The police say the case has grown cold, and they assigned us a case number and abandoned us. Mark is withdrawn. He doesn't talk about Melissa's disappearance. He just works."

"Is he doing any better?" Susan asked.

"Mark..." Barbara paused, thinking how to explain. "...well, let's put it this way, he has his good days and bad days," she finished, wiping away the last remnant of tears from her eyes.

Susan looked at Barbara with concern; she had never seen her in such a fragile state. She hoped things would be different now they were home from their three-week cruise.

Gripping Barbara's shoulders tightly, she sternly announced, "I want all of you to come over for dinner tonight. Don't argue; it's Friday, and no one is working tomorrow, right?"

Knowing she wouldn't win no matter how much she resisted, Barbara nodded her head.

Susan smiled and said, "Surely, you remember John has to eat before six o'clock, or else he turns into a grizzly bear."

"What, little old me?" John interjected. Taking Barbara's hand, he proclaimed, "I still know some of the fellows down at White Plains Police Department. When I get home, the first thing I'm going to do is call an old friend who's a detective at the station to see if they found any new evidence in the case. Don't worry; we're home now."

Susan grabbed hold of the destitute mother, hugging her tightly while saying, "Barbara, you promise me you're coming to the house for dinner."

"Yes, of course, we'll be there. Tell me what we can bring,"

"Just your appetites. Unless you want to bring some dessert?"

"It's the least we can do—tell me, have you heard of that bakery on Smith Street called Godfreys? They make the most delicious cheesecakes."

"Yes, I've heard of them but, you know, since John has diabetes and all, we tend to avoid such places. The truth is I would love some cheesecake; I'll have to make John some sugar-free Jell-O, instead," Susan laughed.

"All right, we'll see you tonight. Love you."

"Please listen, we're home now, and things are going to be different—I promise," John announced.

After a final goodbye the Bernsteins got into their car and drove home. Susan kept her eyes on Barbara until they rounded the corner, then disappeared from sight. Barbara's expression matched her own; they both were feeling the loss of Melissa.

Chapter 2

Entering the house after her friends had gone, Barbara felt a new energy, as if she had had three cups of coffee. She felt a new resolve and purpose. She called Mark at work to tell him the good news. The phone rang a few times and then the sound of someone saying, "Quality Inspection Department."

"Is Mark available? Please tell him his wife is on the phone,"

"Hey Barb, this is Chris. Give me a minute, and I'll see if I can find him. Has anything happened? Do you have news?"

"It's not that important, just tell him to call me when he has time, okay?"

"Speaking of Mark, he just walked in. Here he is."

"Thank you, Chris,"

"This is Mark. Can I help you?"

"Hey honey, it's me."

"What's up, babe?"

"I have some great news: The Bernsteins got back today."

"Great! I suppose that means they received the telegram we sent them. Maybe now, with John's help, we'll be able to get somewhere with Melissa's disappearance."

"Well, you can have that conversation with John tonight over dinner."

"Tonight? Sorry, I already promised Lou that I would come by his house and help him adjust the timing on his pickup. Could we make it another night, perhaps tomorrow?"

"Mark, you know Susan. She insisted we come over tonight. But if you can't make it, then, by all means, give her a call and cancel. I wish you a lot of luck, though." Barbara laughed, trying to sound cheerful.

How could Mark just go help someone with their car? Her life had stopped when Melissa disappeared. Mark's hadn't, and she resented that.

"Hey, forget it. I'd rather tell Lou something's come up so I can't make it. I refuse to be the one who calls Susan. Not me; I'm chicken," Mark chuckled.

"All right, I have to go. I'll see you when you get home from work—l love you."

"Love you, too. Bye."

The rest of the day consisted of laundry and cleaning the house. Before she knew it, it was time to pick Rachel up from school—she hadn't let her come home on the bus since Melissa had disappeared. Quickly gathering her purse and coat, Barbara left home and drove to Jefferson Middle School, where a line of cars waited. As she sat in the car, she had time to ponder the events of the past weeks and felt fortunate her work allowed her to take a leave of absence. Otherwise, missing too many days could result in her losing her job with Bachman and Burns Investment Brokerage Firm.

Devastated by Melissa's disappearance, Barbara could never maintain a friendly, upbeat attitude dealing with clients without breaking down into a weepy mess. Nonetheless, with only a week of her leave remaining, she considered the Bernsteins' return home as an opportunity to ask them if they wouldn't mind picking up Rachel from school.

The loud school bell went off, announcing all the

children were free to leave. Slowly, the classroom doors opened, and groups of children appeared, raced to the waiting cars, and jumped inside. Cars quickly began pulling away, and soon the dash to get out of the confined parking lot began in earnest.

Moments later she spotted a familiar crowd of children. Amid the group she caught a glimpse of Rachel, wearing her bright pink sweater, burdened down with a large backpack. She looked Native American, with features she inherited from Mark's mother—long, dark hair, a dark complexion, and the tallest girl in her class. Melissa resembled Barbara's side of the family, with the Bishops' blonde hair and blue eyes. When Melissa realized her little sister would soon be taller than her, she was upset and constantly measured her height against her sister.

While the crowd of kids hurried along, Rachel looked up and saw her mother sitting in the car so ran to get inside. Opening the door, she threw her backpack on the floor and jumped in. Reaching over and locking the seatbelt into place, she sat still, ready to leave.

"So, how was your day?" Barbara asked, driving away from the crowded school parking lot.

"Boring."

"Boring—what do you mean boring?"

"Nothing exciting ever happens. Oh, I mean mostly nothing. Every day it's the same old stuff. However, Mrs. Krupp sure seemed excited to tell the class that the Berlin Wall fell last night. The Cold War between Berlin's Communist Party and the West is healthier than in times past. I guess that means citizens are now free to cross the country's borders and see their families, becoming united again, no longer apart."

"Yes, I heard that on the radio; they're saying President Reagan was a key player in breaking down the wall.

Anything else?" Barbara asked.

Suddenly, there was an awkward pause, then without any warning Rachel broke out in tears and cried bitterly.

"Mom, will we ever be a family again? Why has Melissa disappeared? Please tell me—what happened to my sister?"

Pulling the car next to the curb, Barbara parked and grabbed her daughter. As she held her warmly, the flood of emotions burst out. This entire time since the kidnapping Rachel had remained silent, never showing any outward response to Melissa's disappearance.

Now, no longer able to hold in her emotions, her desperate child continued to bawl. Barbara was grateful her daughter could finally free herself of this burden. She knew keeping everything inside wasn't right, and soon the effects would surface in ways that weren't healthy.

Barbara made a solemn oath never to give up the fight to find Melissa, no matter how difficult things became.

Staring into her daughter's swollen eyes, she pledged that Melissa would return to them—unharmed.

Rachel looked back and said, "Mom, I hope you're right, but I cannot help but miss my sister."

"I understand, honey. I miss Melissa, too. Hey, listen, you'll never guess who stopped by today."

A moment of silence, then Rachel only shrugged her shoulders.

"John and Susan are back home from their cruise!"

"The Bernsteins are back home!" Rachel shouted excitedly.

"Yes, they arrived just a few hours ago."

"Awesome news—that makes me very happy. Do you have a tissue, Mom? My nose is running."

"Sure, there should be one in the glove box. If not, I'll check my purse,"

"Here's one. Oh—do you need one, too? Your mascara

is running."

"Yes, please check and see if there's enough for both of us."

"I got them; here is one for you."

"Thanks."

Taking the tissue from her daughter, Barbara dabbed the tears from her eyes. A moment later she announced, "Oh, I almost forgot. we need to stop by Godfrey's Bakery to pick up a cheesecake for tonight."

"Yummy, cheesecake."

"Now listen, that's for dessert; I know how you love cheesecake."

"Sure, whatever you say. I love you, Mother."

"I love you, too. Now listen to me. Whoever has taken Melissa will regret the day they were born, I promise you."

"I feel the same way. Whatever it takes to get Melissa back, I'll do it!"

"Well, we don't have much time to get ourselves ready for dinner. Tell me, do you have any homework this weekend?"

"I always have homework, both math and English," Rachel explained sourly.

"Well, you'll have to bring it with you."

"I already started some of it during my study period."

"Good, I have a feeling tonight is going to be a whirlwind."

"Please never leave me, okay? I love you, Mom, but you already know that."

"Regardless, I never grow tired of hearing it, and neither does your father. We never try to forget to express our love to one another because you never know if something horrible could happen to us. That day when Melissa left for school, she and I said, 'I love you.' I'm so glad, and even now, I feel her spirit alive within my heart."

"Mom, I know we used to say bad things to each other, but I still love her and always will."

"I don't doubt it. Now, will you look at the time? We have to get going. I'm not sure how bad traffic will be downtown."

Quickly slipping the car into drive, she drove away with Rachel. Although still emotionally distraught, Rachel's attitude seemed optimistic.

Looking at the time, Barbara realized they would be late getting to the Bernsteins' house for dinner, but for a good reason. Things in life come at you unexpectedly, and when they do, you have no choice but to deal with them.

When they arrived at Godfrey's Bakery, they bailed out of the car and ran inside. A small line had formed in front of the glass display case. A baker was helping an older woman. Next in line was a man and his wife. As they waited, Barbara had time to eye her selection. There behind the glass was a cheesecake decorated with strawberries on top.

That one will do nicely, she thought, *unless someone buys it.*

Soon came their turn; Barbara pointed to her choice, and a moment later they were back in the car, headed for home. When they arrived, Barbara saw Mark's truck parked in front of the garage. She hoped he was ready to go but, knowing her husband, she doubted it. Walking into the house, she saw he was sitting on the couch, watching a boxing match on television and only made aware of their arrival when he saw Rachel running to her bedroom.

Barbara appeared in front of the television, blocking Mark's view.

"I thought you would be ready to go to the Bernsteins'?" she said.

"Hey, I already showered and got dressed. Let's go; I'm just waiting for you."

"You're not going to wear that old stained sweatshirt, are you?"

"I suppose not."

"All right, I just need to freshen up a little, and we'll be on our way," Barbara announced.

Staring intently at his wife and noticing her red eyes, he said, "I see you've been crying. Is there something I need to know?"

"Please, I'm running late. Can we talk about it in the car? I'll be happy to tell you about it then."

"Sure, at least give me a hint of the subject matter?"

"It's about Rachel. Today when I picked her up from school, she had an emotional breakdown."

"What? Tough as nails Rachel, no! I have a real hard time believing that! Now I'm afraid I'll be the one calling the Bernsteins to tell them we're running late. Sit down. I want to hear all about it."

"Nothing much to tell, really. From the expression on Rachel's face, I could see something was troubling her. All I did was ask her about her day, and she talked about the Berlin Wall coming down and the families reunited. Then bam, she lost it. You know the truth is, ever since Melissa has disappeared, Rachel's been forgotten and pushed aside."

"Yes, I know. I was afraid of this happening, but what could we do? All of our resources have been spent on finding Melissa and nothing else. Hell, we hardly communicate ourselves, notwithstanding Rachel and her needs."

"I'm as guilty as you, but from now on we need to pay close attention to our daughter, or else some creep out there will. I don't need to say anything else, do I?"

"No, you're coming through, loud and clear. Now get your butt ready while I call Susan."

"Look, I'm already gone."

"Didn't the Bernsteins just get home today from their

trip, and now they want us to come over for dinner?"

"Yes, but you know Susan. There's just no arguing with her. Shoot, look at the time. We're supposed to be there in less than an hour."

Without argument Mark quickly turned off the TV, went into their bedroom, and put on a clean shirt. He left, promising to call Susan as Barbara remained behind to freshen up. Taking a small amount of cologne and spraying her neck, she scrutinized her image in the mirror.

Unexpectedly, something flashed behind her reflection. Was something dark moving behind her? She spun around to see what it was—nothing was there, just the darkness of the walk-in closet a few feet away. Moving carefully toward the door to leave, she passed through a frigid air pocket directly in front of her, which sent a shiver up her spine.

Instinctively, Barbara moved backward, away from the invisible phenomenon that blocked her exit. She stood near the door, breathing heavily, and stared forward. She saw nothing out of the ordinary. Strange, the rest of the room seemed pleasant—all except for that pocket of coldness.

Without evidence of something being there, she shook her head and quickly dismissed the strange sensation as a problem with a heater duct. Taking another look at herself in the mirror, she thought, *This is ridiculous. We have to get to the Bernsteins' house. I have no time to waste on my imagination getting the better of me.*

Determined to escape, she walked out of the bathroom and shut off the light behind her. Safely inside her bedroom, she momentarily hesitated and stood perfectly still, not moving.

Bravely, turning back around, she reached inside the dark bathroom. There was nothing out of the ordinary; the space seemed as warm as the rest of the house.

What on earth am I doing. This is silly.

To some degree, it was strange, though, for as soon as

she pulled away. Something—yes—something invisible from within reached out and tapped the top of her hand, sending shivers down her spine. As quickly as she could, she withdrew her hand and screamed.

From the living room, Mark yelled out, "Are you okay? You didn't burn yourself with your curling iron again, did you?"

"No, I'm fine,"

Racing out of the bedroom, she appeared next to Mark, gripping her purse tightly, and said, "I'm ready, let's go—now!"

"Sure thing, whatever you say," Mark responded, surprised by his wife's need to make a hasty departure.

Chapter 3

A short time later after locking the house, Mark looked around him to see where Barbara had gone, then glanced at his wife's car in the driveway. There she was in the passenger seat, staring ahead, waiting for him nervously.

That is strange. Usually I'm the one sitting in the car blowing my horn for Barbara to hurry, he thought. *Something's going on that she's not telling me.*

He and Rachel got in the car and headed out.

"Hon, are we having problems with our furnace?"

"What? Our furnace? Not that I'm aware of. Why?"

"Oh, no reason, I suppose. It's just when I was in the bathroom getting ready, I felt a strange pocket of frigid air."

"You see? Again, my argument for wanting to purchase a new home instead of that old, dilapidated house you inherited from your father. It would be far wiser than wasting our money on repairs each month on that piece of junk."

"Whatever, Mark. You're wasting your breath. I'm not ready to begin making large monthly payments so you can brag to your friends at work that you have a new house. I'd rather spend our money on the girls' college fund."

"The girls, you say. I believe you forget we're one shy of a complete family?" Mark barked.

"Mark, forget it. Everything with you is an argument."

Silence, blissful silence, and no one spoke the remainder of the drive. Arriving at the Bernstein residence, Mark walked up and rang the doorbell. John appeared and greeted everyone warmly. Once inside, John asked if anyone cared for a drink.

"Sure, I'll take a beer if you have one," Mark answered.

"Yes, I'll have a scotch on the rocks. Thanks, John," Barbara responded. Walking into the kitchen, Barbara found Susan at the stove, preparing dinner.

A few minutes later John appeared and said, "Here's your scotch, Barb."

He handed her a decorative glass with ice; Barbara took a long swig.

After setting down the glass, Susan asked, "Barb, did you have a bad day or something?"

"I'm better now. Thank you, John.

Turning to Susan, she replied, "It's just stress and all," not revealing the truth about what happened in their bathroom.

"Oh sweetie, both John and I understand. Could you please help me with the salad?"

"Yes, of course,"

Soon both she and Rachel joined in and were cutting vegetables, leaving the men to talk sports.

John returned to the living room and stared at Mark.

"Mark, have you noticed anything strange about Barbara lately? I've never seen her drink scotch."

"Yeah, she seemed a little spooked when we left the house, saying something about our heater malfunctioning or something like that."

"Hum, that is strange," John announced.

"Yeah, what are you going to do, right?"

Mark, a frequent guest, quickly made himself comfortable on the couch. Seeing a baseball game on the television, he turned to John and asked, "What inning is it?"

Still troubled by Barbara's nervousness, John explained,

"It's the top of the seventh; the Boston Red Sox are leading the Yankees, five to three." Suddenly paying attention to the game, a New York Yankee struck out; it pleased John greatly.

Grabbing the remote, John unexpectedly shut off the television, turned to Mark, and said, "I called the police station today to see if any new details were discovered in Melissa's case."

"Did you learn anything new?"

"All I can tell you is the lieutenant who's handling Melissa's case is one of the best," John explained as a way of easing Mark's worries. "Everything humanly possible is being done to find Melissa."

Mark, hoping for more, sat back in his seat and stared down at the floor, and John changed the subject, ranting about the difficulties of getting through customs and canceling the rest of their cruise.

Having just arrived in a foreign country, it was difficult for them to suddenly change their itinerary. The mere cost of changing flights was astronomical, and the connections between flights—forget it—the waiting and communication problems at Soviet airports, particularly one named Pulkovo, was most troublesome.

Mark tried his best to be courteous; a haunting absence in his life robbed him of any emotion. His mind wandered, and he found himself daydreaming of happy times with Melissa. He remembered one time in particular when they had come over to the Bernsteins' house after Melissa's softball team won the league championship.

Melissa had insisted on showing them her trophy. She'd been so excited she couldn't sit still. Mark remembered telling her to calm down as she spoke a mile a minute, explaining how her best friend had caught the ball that won the game.

Susan and John had encouraged Melissa to tell them everything about that day and not leave out any details. Remembering that happy moment, Mark looked over at John, with whom he felt a closeness, and silently watched him babbling about his experiences. How lucky they were to have such friends who shared their grief and knew their loss.

Mark felt that Melissa's abductor must have had a good idea of her routine and schedule. *How else could they have known where she would be at any particular moment?* However, the timing of her disappearance didn't make any sense. *If she was in school, as she should have been, why didn't any kids see her get taken?* He knew his daughter, and she wouldn't just give up without a fight.

Maybe that's why the police had found a piece of Melissa's sweater. Perhaps she'd fought her abductors with all the strength she could muster. *Oh, I hope that's true*, Mark thought. Imagining his daughter somehow fighting her abductors made him feel better about the situation. Still, Melissa was just a teenage girl.

How much damage could she inflict upon an adult male? If indeed a man was involved. He and his daughter were close; they'd spent a lot of time in wilderness training together through the Girl Scouts. Mark hoped she was safe and protected from harm. Why would anyone want to hurt her?

As he considered what could have happened, a new line of reasoning occurred to him. *Unless it was someone Melissa felt safe with, it had to be someone she trusted, or she would have run away as quickly as her legs could carry her. Her abductor would've needed lots of luck to catch her; she's as swift as a cheetah and could even outrun me in a footrace.*

His thoughts were suddenly interrupted by the appearance of Barbara coming from the kitchen, announcing that dinner was ready. John didn't acknowledge her but continued talking about their troubles getting back through customs. He'd not heard a word she had said.

Looking up, Mark replied softly, "I'll tell him dinner is ready."

Barbara stood there silently for a minute, seeing if John would even acknowledge her, but he remained fixated on his storytelling. She thought, *How could John be so engrossed in telling his problems is beyond me.* Discouraged, Barbara turned around and went back into the kitchen to help Susan.

Disgusted, she asked Susan, "Is John always so absorbed in details as he is now? I told the boys that dinner's ready, and John didn't even hear a word I said."

Susan laughed and replied, "Now you know how John is when it comes to accurate details. He can't help himself, especially when he's describing a story involving laws and customs." Susan took off her apron and laid it on the counter. "I'll get him," she boasted.

Walking into the living room, she abruptly yelled at the top of her lungs, "Dinner is ready!" causing John to jump several inches out of his seat.

Mark and Barbara laughed while John did his best to recover from the shock. He got up from his chair and walked into the kitchen, grumbling. Sitting at the kitchen table, he scowled back at Susan in response.

Trying to think of a way to console his pouting friend, Mark asked, "John, tell me, how's the Boston Red Sox doing this year? Do you think they'll make it to the world series?"

The question quickly changed John's mood as he eagerly explained the Red Sox were getting close to winning their division. As they talked about baseball, Susan brought over a steaming pot of spaghetti, which she placed in the middle of the table.

"Dig in," Susan announced.

As they all followed her advice, John said, "I want to

suggest we get together tomorrow to make up some fliers with Melissa's picture and staple them on every telephone pole around town."

Mark swiftly protested. "There's no reason to go into that again; they did that when Melissa first went missing, with no success."

"I realize you tried that already, but this time I want to offer a reward. Susan and I agree the sum of ten thousand dollars to anyone with information leading to Melissa's safe return will have favorable results."

Barbara turned to look at Mark for some answer or approval, but she could only see resentment brewing on his face. The last time they'd tried something like that it hadn't worked and left both of them discouraged.

"John, we already tried that before, and we didn't have any favorable success then. What makes you think your idea will work out differently?"

John thought for a moment before responding, then he looked at the parents lovingly and spoke. "Because I'm offering real hard cash, that's the difference. I know people you might consider immoral. These people will do almost anything for the amount of reward I'm offering,"

Growing excited, Barbara asked, "What do you mean, John?"

"Let me just say this: I have friends in high places," John announced, looking smug as he wiped sauce from his mouth.

Mark and Susan both looked unconvinced.

Noticing their skepticism, John replied, "Oh, ye of little faith."

"That's just great," Susan said. "Did you ever think for one minute that maybe Mark and Barbara didn't want to go through the headache of having strangers prowling around looking for clues?"

"This is different," John answered. "I plan on showing

Melissa's picture to a select few individuals who have connections across the country."

"I think it's a superb idea, John," Barbara replied. "I've always felt Melissa's abductors couldn't be from around here. They're probably living somewhere else, far away. Don't ask me why I think that; it's just what I believe."

Having settled on giving John's idea a try, they all sat around the living room and tried to talk about other things, such as the Bernsteins' cruise. Still, the conversation always came back to Melissa's disappearance. Soon everyone was yawning.

Mark looked at his watch and tiredly said, "It's late. We'd better be going home."

Barbara was so comfortable on the sofa that she could have slept there all night, curled up under the soft throw wrapped around her body. "Go ahead without me," she responded with her eyelids half-closed.

"Come on, babe. We've got to go."

Grudgingly, with Mark's help, Barbara raised herself to her feet and walked over to their daughter, who had fallen asleep in a chair, and tenderly announced, "Come, Rachel, it's time to go."

After saying their goodbyes to John and Susan, they headed home. On the way Mark publicized his disapproval of Barbara's agreement to have some "nut jobs," as he called them, looking into Melissa's disappearance. He didn't see the need for going through "all of that bullshit" all over again.

"I'm willing to try anything," Barbara responded. "I'm sure it's not bullshit; you know John and what a good investigator he was at the U.S. Marshals office. He won countless accolades for solving missing person's cases. Besides, if he's willing to help us find Melissa, I'm ready to try anything that will bring her back home. I'm just surprised by your reluctance."

Rachel listened to her parents as they argued back and forth. She didn't express her thoughts on the subject. All that mattered to her was that someone, whoever it was, find her sister.

Her parents never knew she had overheard Jessica from school telling everyone that she had seen the people who had kidnapped Melissa. Rachel hadn't said anything to either of them since she doubted it was true. After all, Jessica was known for telling tall tales. Jessica bragged her family would soon be wealthy after discovering a buried treasure of gold and that her parents had agreed that when they became rich they would buy her a pony after they moved into their mansion. She would invite all of her friends to go swimming in her pool.

When they finally reached home, Mark parked the car in the garage; Rachel was the first to run into the house. She wanted to escape attention while her parents continued their quarreling. Rachel had grown accustomed to being the family's unspoken member of the household. She lived in Melissa's shadow, where nobody paid her any attention—at times feeling unimportant. To her, that wasn't ever going to change, which was fine.

After walking down the dark hallway that led to her room, Rachel passed by Melissa's doorway and thought she saw something move in the shadows. Stopping in her tracks, she stared into the darkness, expecting to see something move. Instead, she experienced a cold blast of air coming from the bedroom, drifting outward into the hallway. Goosebumps raised all over her skin. Expecting to see a reason for the coldness, she waited and gazed inside, but nothing moved.

Just then, her attention was diverted by her parents' argument moving inside the house. Taking one last look into the darkness, she saw nothing strange or different and continued to her room. After closing the door to her private retreat, she got prepared for bed while her parents' argument raged on.

Not gaining any ground on the matter, Mark said, "I know John will try his best, but even he can only do so much. I miss Melissa; I can still hear her laughter. It haunts me during the night." He began to sob uncontrollably.

Barbara quietly walked over and held him tightly, allowing him to release the pent-up stress and anger he could no longer contain.

After a few minutes he pulled himself away and said, "I'm so damn frustrated. You know the type of man I am; give me a mountain, tell me to climb it, no problem. I feel sick to my stomach as I wait for the inevitable phone call that will tell us they found Melissa's body in a trash dumpster or discarded along the road somewhere."

"Mark, I know how you feel, but I don't want you to give up on our daughter. I will continue to fight as long as there is breath within me."

He stepped away slightly and said, "I haven't given up, either, dammit."

"I didn't say you had. I'm just thrilled John and Susan are home to help us. Maybe we can finally get the support we need. In my heart I believe Melissa is still alive and, for some reason, I imagine a sinister force behind it all."

"Barbara, what are you saying? What menacing force is behind this abduction besides some sick, twisted mind? I think you've been reading too many mystery novels."

"I know it sounds strange," Barbara admitted, "but the other day when I was making dinner, I swear I heard Melissa calling my name,"

"Hon, that's odd," Mark replied. "But it's getting late, and I need to be going to bed." He yawned and added, "I'm feeling quite tired."

"Sure, go ahead," Barbara replied. "I just want to clean up in the kitchen for a bit, and I'll be right there."

Saying good night, she kissed her husband and turned back toward the kitchen. After she had finished tidying up, she made her way to bed. Yes, it would've been the perfect time to tell Mark about the strange experience she had in her bathroom earlier, but in his state of mind she doubted he would believe her. No, it was best to discuss the strange happenings in the morning over breakfast.

When she arrived in their bedroom, Mark was already snoring. After changing into her pajamas, she went into the bathroom to remove her makeup. Afterward, she crawled into bed and shut off the lamp. She was grateful that this time she felt no strange coldness in their bathroom. Clearly, nothing more than a clogged air vent.

While she lay there staring up at the ceiling, restless and unable to relax, the reality of John offering such a large reward made her feel guilty. Still, hearing Mark's rhythmic breathing made sleep unavoidable. Finally, Barbara drifted off to sleep.

All remained quiet throughout the house except for the humming of the refrigerator in the kitchen. A distant dog let out a nervous bark. Barbara realized she had forgotten to close the drapes of their large bedroom window.

As she stared out into the backyard at the giant oak tree, the shadows cast by the moonlight slowly moved across the grass, allowing its leaves to flitter with the gentle passing breeze.

Unexpectedly, the image before her changed. She noticed something crawling from underneath the tree roots: a gray-haired rabbit hopped onto the yard's green surface. It squatted there, oblivious of her presence. Its large, floppy ears and paws remained motionless; only its nose wiggled back and forth. It seemed to be chewing on something, which she guessed was probably their manicured lawn.

Rabbits were a problem, she thought. Mark tried his best to eradicate the pest, which had ruined their lawn and shrubs in the past, but he'd had little success. However, this rabbit had suddenly shown up on their turf, unwelcome, and sat staring at her, unmoving. It must be feeling brave.

She wanted to wake Mark from his sleep and send him outside to get the critter. Instead, she just watched the rabbit stare back at her as it munched on her green lawn. "Of all the audacity," she mused. "This little creature takes the cake." He didn't move or seem frightened or shy about being out in the open while he stared back at her, chewing.

Suddenly, a menacing black shadow appeared, circling above the rabbit, yet the rabbit didn't move or run away. It remained eating, staring, defiant, and unwavering. Without warning a pair of dark, razor-sharp talons appeared in a flashing image before Barbara's eyes, carried by two black wings that appeared and then vanished into the night sky. She turned back to look at the rabbit and saw its body had been ripped open, and its heart and entrails were missing. Oblivious to what had happened to it, the rabbit continued chewing.

The sight frightened her, but she remained curious and watched with great interest. Without warning the rabbit stopped chewing. It opened its mouth slowly, and out came a shiny object that Barbara recognized as belonging to Melissa. It was a locket Barbara had given her on her sixteenth birthday. A family heirloom, it had once belonged to Barbara's grandmother.

Barbara shot up out of bed and screamed out loud, "Melissa," waking Mark.

"What is it?" he responded, not knowing where he was.

Barbara, now fully awake, stared at the clock: The time read ten minutes past midnight. Taking a moment to calm herself, she thought, *I'm never going to get any sleep now.* Getting up from the bed, she went to the kitchen to get a glass of water. Reluctantly, she returned to their bedroom, knowing she would end up staring at the ceiling for another hour before exhaustion overtook her, and then dawn would appear too quickly.

Passing by Melissa's bedroom, she turned on the light and looked inside. On her daughter's dresser stood a picture of Melissa at her sixteenth birthday party when Barbara had given her the necklace—the same necklace she saw in her nightmare. What did the dream mean? Was it symbolic? After turning off the light, she returned to her room and crawled back under the sheets. Now haunted by the nightmare of the rabbit torn apart, sleep eluded her for a brief time. But soon exhaustion had its effects, and she fell fast asleep.

The following day Barbara opened her eyes and looked at the clock near her bed: The large red numbers displayed six thirty-five a.m. She didn't usually get up so early on a Saturday morning, but the nightmare from the night before still left her feeling disturbed. Grudgingly, Barbara surrendered to the beginning of a new day and got up to make breakfast. Slowly crawling out of bed, she tried her best not to wake Mark.

She traveled down the long hallway toward the kitchen to make coffee. Passing by Melissa's room, she paused and peeped inside. The room hadn't been disturbed since the day her daughter disappeared. The empty bed lay there with the sheets crudely pulled over the mattress and pillow, along with two of Melissa's favorite stuffed animals lifelessly guarding the room.

Barbara cautiously stepped into the bedroom and made her way over to Melissa's soft mattress. Quietly, she lay down on the bed and rested her head on her daughter's pillow.

Barbara surveyed Melissa's belongings through the dim morning light in the peaceful surroundings and looked at the many pictures, primarily famous teen idols, pinned on the walls.

On her dresser was a portrait of the family, all dressed in red for their annual Christmas grouping. Wallet-sized pictures of her school friends were stuck between the frame and glass of the large dresser mirror, complete with beaded necklaces and feathers cascading down the side.

The room felt cold as if a window had been left open. Still, there was a tranquil quietness that begged Barbara to stay. She imagined the sounds of Melissa's laughter haunting the small space. Countless memories flooded the room. She wanted to absorb as many of them as she could. Some memories brought a smile, others a frown or a tear.

A mother's bond with her child is never-ending. No one else can know the depths of that love or what a mother is willing to do for their child.

Unexpectedly, Mark appeared in the hallway. Respecting his wife's moment of reflection, he remained quietly still. Standing there, he could hear her sobbing, alone on their daughter's bed, clutching one of Melissa's favorite stuffed animals as her tears flowed down her cheeks.

Without words he lay down beside her, embracing her tightly. He felt helpless at seeing his wife in such a state of despair and wished there was something he could do for her. But at that moment the only thing she needed from him was to be held and comforted, which he did with all the love he could give.

His warm body and thoughtful response soothed her, and she reached over and pulled him close. In the comfort of one another's arms, they spent the next few hours absorbing the loss of their daughter.

A short time later Rachel awoke. Instinctively heading

down the hallway toward the kitchen, she was startled to see her parents in Melissa's bedroom, lying on the bed. Still partly asleep, she quickly cuddled up between them, closer to her mother.

A few moments later she stared up at Barbara and said, "What's for breakfast?"

"What would you like to eat this morning?" Barbara asked, twirling her daughter's long, thick black hair around her finger.

Rachel, of course, suggested pancakes.

Mark laughed and asked, "Is there ever a time you want something else besides pancakes for breakfast?"

Giggling at her father's comment, Rachel said, "I like how Mom decorates happy faces on them with the whipped cream, and they taste so good, better than when you make them, Dad."

Hearing this, Mark said, "Come here, you turkey." He reached down and took ahold of Rachel's foot and began to tickle her madly.

Kicking legs and loud screaming changed the somber mood Barbara had felt earlier, and she laughed.

"All right, you two, I guess it must be time to get up since you can't behave yourselves."

Laughing, again unexpectedly, she rose from the bed while Rachel continued to beg for mercy from her father's tickling. Once free, Rachel reached over to her Dad, tapped him on the head, proclaimed he was it, and then ran out of the bedroom, wanting to be chased.

Unfortunately, Mark was too tired to give pursuit. He laughed aloud and rose from the bed, following Barbara into the kitchen to make the morning coffee. After a few minutes the coffee maker's alarm sounded, and he turned and asked, "Are you ready for a cup?"

"Yes, please, I'll add my creamer, though. You always

put too much in."

"Hey, I just make it as I like it."

Again, thank you, but I'll add my creamer. Besides, breakfast will be ready soon, and the dog still needs to be fed. I'm busy cooking."

"All over it," Mark responded.

The phone rang, and Mark turned to her and said, "I wonder who that could be."

"Not, sure who'll be calling us this early, but I'll answer it. Please go and feed the dog."

When Barbara answered the phone, she wasn't surprised to hear Susan on the other end of the receiver. ,

"Good morning, Barb, do you have a minute?"

"Yes, Susan, what's up?"

"Barbara, listen to me. I don't want anyone knowing the reason for my call. I haven't told John I was calling you, and please don't tell Mark, okay? I don't believe they'd understand. Just listen to what I have to say. I'm sure it will sound nutty at first, but, believe me, no one else I know has tried anything like this before."

Looking behind her, she saw Mark had left the kitchen and went outside into the garage.

"I'm alone. Tell me about your idea."

"Okay, please keep an open mind, all right?"

"Yes, of course. Susan, would you just tell me!"

"Now, listen, years ago I remember a case John was working on that involved a missing little girl. The bureau hired a man by the name of Sterling to investigate her disappearance,"

"What makes him so special?"

"He's a psychic detective. Can you believe it? I thought I'd heard of everything, but I remember how impressed John was to have him on the case."

"Come on, Susan. You know Mark and I don't believe in

that stuff,"

"Well, you should start believing because this Sterling character found that missing girl."

"He did? Tell me, was she still alive?"

"Yes, now listen. I have to go but you need to give it some thought—okay? That's all I'm saying. Shoot, I have to go. I hear John pulling up in the driveway. Talk to you later. Goodbye,"

"Susan, before you go, is it possible you could watch Rachel after school? It'll only be for an hour or so. I wanted to ask sooner but with everything…."

"I would be upset if you didn't ask. Besides, I already have that time marked on the calendar. Both John and I realize you have to return to work; it only seems natural. We'll talk more. I have to be going,"

Immediately, the receiver went dead.

A psychic. I'm beginning to believe Susan is losing it—a psychic of all things, Barbara thought. Hanging up the phone, she returned to the stove and saw her eggs were burned to a crisp.

Just then Mark appeared in the kitchen and asked, "What did Susan want?"

"Oh, you know. They're having a sale on tomatoes down at the market,"

"That's odd. They just arrived home from their trip and already she's telling you about tomatoes being on sale."

"You know Susan; she's thrifty if nothing else," Barbara muttered.

"Sure, I suppose," Mark answered and walked away.

"A psychic detective," Barbara whispered to herself, "What are the possibilities?"

Surprisingly, she felt a fire ignite inside as she pondered strange questions. Did that type of thing exist? Could a man have the ability to see into the past or future and interpret plausible shreds of evidence and minuscule signs that have been overlooked by everyone else? Barbara wasn't sure what it all meant, but she also couldn't accept her child's fate and surrender to the inevitable.

No, never has it been written down in the annals of time that a mother has accepted her child's disappearance and continued with her life as if nothing had happened. Why now? Should this moment in time be any different than those that have come before her? Whoever has taken Melissa better prepare themselves for war.

Chapter 4

Startled awake by the alarm's early Monday morning broadcast, Barbara reached over and punched the snooze button. Pulling the sheets up over her head, she covered her face, hoping for another minute or two of blissful sleep. Nevertheless, the ringing alarm reminded her of the many things she needed to accomplish. She hadn't fully awakened when she started to move. Regardless of how warm and comfortable the soft bed felt, she had to get up.

She rose to her feet with half-open eyelids and went into the bathroom, turned on the hot water in the shower and, a minute later, forced herself to get inside. The soothing hot water began to wake her, allowing her mind to drift. She thought about John offering such a large amount of money and wondered about his so-called sources. Hopefully, John's contacts could find Melissa so their lives would return to normal and finally, she and Mark could wake up from this nightmare.

Not wanting to be late for her first day back to the office, she brushed her thoughts aside and quickly finished washing. In the next room Mark was still asleep. She tried to get ready quickly but was still running later than she hoped. Rachel would only hinder her efforts, each school day a struggle.

When Barbara appeared in Rachel's bedroom to wake

her for school, the first words out of her mouth were: "Mom, can I stay home today?"

"Do you feel sick?"

"Well…" Rachel had never been able to lie very well so tried to think of an excuse.

"Then why do you want to stay home?"

Rachel hung her head and mumbled that her science homework wasn't completed.

"You should've told me you were having problems last night when I could've helped you," Barbara said. "Now go get dressed."

She pointed toward Rachel's closet, and the child crawled out of bed and reluctantly got herself dressed for school.

Once Rachel was safely on the bus, Barbara had only minutes to spare before she had to leave for work. Now she had her job to consider. It had been hard enough trying to preserve any normalcy in her life, but juggling work and family life after Melissa's abduction was going to be nearly impossible.

Arriving at work, she put her lunch away in the refrigerator before heading to her desk with a large cup of coffee. She began sorting through her many emails and looked over her schedule for the day. There were only a few meetings so she was free to catch up on her filing and organizing. The day passed quickly, and as she was leaving the office she remembered she had a five-thirty appointment with her therapist. Again, running behind, she raced to the parking garage and hurriedly drove away.

Arriving downtown for her appointment with Dr. Melbourne, Barbara quickly parked the car. After grabbing her purse, she hurried to the entrance, pushed through the glass doors, and clambered up the stairs, stopping at the small office door marked 212. After walking inside,

Barbara signed in for her appointment and greeted the receptionist.

"Hello, Pam, I made it on time, a little touch and go, but here I am."

Walking toward a group of stuffed chairs, she removed her coat and sat down. Glancing at her watch, she was surprised to discover she was early. *Nothing to do but wait,* she thought. In front of her on the decorative glass table was an assortment of magazines.

Choosing a science magazine, she opened it and began reading an article announcing an astronomical occurrence for later that month. The report publicized details about the moon shadowing an eclipse four times in a row—a blood moon. The term meant a full moon of a lunar tetrad that came from the eerie reddish glow such eclipses characteristically gave off. The last one had occurred between CE 1493 and 1494.

Just then the solid mahogany door to the waiting room swung open. A woman, someone Barbara hadn't seen before, walked up to the receptionist to make her next appointment. Pam handed the woman a small card, and she left. A short time later the receptionist received an alert on her computer.

"The doctor will see you now," she said.

Gathering her belongings, Barbara hurried inside. Walking past the wooden glass doors and down the hall, she hesitated briefly before going in. Lately, her therapist had begun to ask personal questions, almost to the point of being intrusive. Yes, understandably so, it was needed to get at the source of Barbara's unhappiness. Still, the answer seemed clear to her: Find Melissa, and all would be right again. Now, however, she was left with an emptiness that couldn't be filled.

The only way to come to terms with Melissa's

abduction was to bring her emotional state out in the open. But still, at times, the therapist's line of questioning was a bit much.

Gathering up her courage, she went inside. At her desk Dr. Melbourne was busily examining Barbara's chart. Wearing a pleasant smile, the fifty-something doctor asked Barbara to sit in either of the two cushioned chairs in the room. Studying the doctor, Barbara noticed the absence of a wedding ring on her finger. Sitting on her desk was a picture of a miniature Schnauzer. Upon the walls were doctorate degrees of completion but no family pictures—most likely a professional who chose her career over having a family.

Unexpectedly, Dr. Melbourne looked up and asked, "Are you comfortable?"

"Yes, thank you."

Walking away from her desk and taking the adjacent chair next to Barbara, Dr. Melbourne herself sat down and began writing something down in her notepad. A moment later she asked, "How was your day?"

Feeling hesitant to go into great detail, Barbara said, "Today was my first day back to work. There was nothing out of the ordinary, just getting caught up on my emails, reviewing client activities, and scheduling meetings for my director."

Dr. Melbourne asked about Barbara's emotional state throughout her day. "Are you having any difficulties at work that could be connected to Melissa's disappearance?"

"To tell you the truth, I was terrified every time the phone rang. I almost certainly expect it to be the police department calling to tell me they had found Melissa's body in a ditch somewhere. Throughout my day it was a constant worry."

The doctor listened as Barbara began to open up about

her emotional state. "I'm living a nightmare I just want to wake up from!" she exclaimed.

Dr. Melbourne, apparently expecting the waterworks, grabbed a box of tissues and sat it next to Barbara. Staring silently at the carton, Barbara hesitated. Surprisingly, she realized a weakness in her character. A harsh reality struck her. Each time she thought of Melissa, the results were the same: She broke down into a weeping mess. She wished she was more assertive, but she didn't know where to begin. Somewhere, deep within her, was a hidden strength she knew she had, but how could she find it?

Without warning the doctor asked, "How was your life before Melissa's abduction?"

Somewhat surprised by the inquiry, Barbara replied, "We were a happy family. Mark is patient, kind, an excellent father for the girls."

The doctor paused and then wrote down more notes on her small pad and asked, "Why did you choose to tell me that Mark is an excellent father? I find it interesting you would bring that point up."

"Okay, well, I believe some people in White Plains blame both Mark and me for Melissa's disappearance. There have been rumors about Mark's temper; some townspeople, including the police, wonder if there was foul play involved," Barbara explained.

"Let me ask you something, Barbara. Has Mark ever been abusive toward you or your daughters?"

"Never!" Barbara exclaimed. "I'm surprised you would even ask me such a question."

Surprisingly, their half-hour session went by too quickly. Just outside, another patient was waiting. Dr. Melbourne finished writing on her pad and looked up at Barbara, suggesting that she write down her thoughts in a diary. At their next appointment they would discuss those issues further.

Agreeing, Barbara took out her checkbook and wrote out a check for her visit. She paused before signing it. Staring at Dr. Melbourne, she announced, "Wait a minute. Something, I cannot tell you what it is, but something inside me feels different."

"Different? Tell me, what you mean?"

"Well, when I saw you reach for that box of tissues, supposing I would need it, your assumptions were upsetting to me or, should I say, pissed me off! I realize that in our brief time together I have broken down, bawling my eyes out. The need to release my inner depression and sadness leads me to realize a weakness in my character. Why does it have to be me alone? Damn it, where's Mark in all of this? Where are my friends? Why am I the only one needing a therapist?"

Surprised by Barbara's outburst, the doctor said, "Could it be you have discovered a remedy of sorts to assist you in managing your daughter's disappearance?"

"If what you're telling me is that being shown my weak frailty in a way I've never seen before, then yes, I suppose you're right. I have discovered something about myself. I'm not the frail woman everyone thinks I am. I will never surrender to the forces that stole my daughter. I realize there's a deep-seated determination within me that is unwilling to surrender. I will find my Melissa!"

Closing her notepad, Dr. Melbourne said, "I believe there's nothing more I can do for you."

"You know something? I believe you're right."

Signing the check, Barbara ripped it from the small book and handed it over. Gathering her belongings, she turned to leave.

Unexpectedly, Dr. Melbourne said, "Barbara, few patients of mine ever experience an epiphany such as yours. Most go on throughout their lives hoping for a spiritual awakening, but sadly, they never find it. Equipped with your newfound strength, go search for your daughter and never give up."

"Thank you for your help, Doctor."

"I only listened; you were the one who unlocked your new abilities. I wish you all the luck in the world, but if at the end of your journey you discover something unfathomable, I'll always be here if you need me."

Nothing left to say, Barbara took her belongings and walked out.

As she passed the receptionist, Pam announced, "Are you ready to schedule your next appointment?"

"No. Sorry, Pam, I'm afraid that won't be necessary. I don't plan on returning."

"Great, I'm glad to hear Dr. Melbourne could help you!"

"Sure, if you want to call it that, go ahead. Either way, you'll not see me again,"

Arriving at her car, Barbara felt a new determination. As she opened her car door, she paused and thought, *Was it the doctor's real purpose to upset me, or perhaps it was a hidden inner strength that needed awakening?* Unsure of the reason for her newfound fortitude, she stared up at the building's glass windows, knowing she would never see the inside of that office again. Perhaps a thank you was in order. But regardless, soon the check would be cashed, and in her mind that is appreciation enough.

Chapter 5

Mark had a lodge meeting after work. She wasn't in the mood to make dinner and decided she would take Rachel out to grab a bite; it would be good for them to have some quiet time together. Earlier that day Barbara had received a message from Lieutenant Reed, the lead investigating detective on Melissa's case. Instead of returning his call, she decided it would be best to visit the police department herself, but she wanted to call Susan first.

Walking back inside the psychiatrist's office building, she found a payphone. Barbara reached inside her purse, took out a quarter, and slipped it into the coin slot. Dialing the Bernsteins' number, she waited.

"Hello, this is Susan. Can I help you?"

"Susan, this is Barb; I have a favor to ask you. Do you think it would be all right if I'm a little late picking up Rachel? I realize this is an inconvenience, but I wanted to stop by the police station. Earlier today Detective Reed left me a message, and I wanted to see if they found out anything new on the case."

"Sure, that will be fine. Rachel's doing her homework; both she and John have been enjoying my chocolate chip cookies,"

"Please tell her not to ruin her appetite; later this evening I plan on taking her out for dinner."

"Oh, she'll be happy to hear that! All right, we'll see you when you get here."

"Susan, I want you to know how appreciative I am that you're watching Rachel. I don't know what Mark and I would do without you and John."

"Listen, no worries. Go see Detective Reed, and be assured Rachel is safe here with us. I promise."

"All right, thank you again. Bye."

On her way to the police station, she had time to consider all the past week's events, including the struggles and hardships. Mark believed her constant interactions with the police were an annoyance. Sure, he wanted to hear some good news about Melissa, but he felt his wife was beating herself up over their daughter's disappearance. He'd even said he had grown worried that she was becoming obsessed to the point where she couldn't think of anything else in her life. Again, she had the feeling that she was alone in this fight.

The traffic was light, and she arrived at the station in no time. However, finding a parking space was another matter. Eventually finding one at the back of the lot, she parked her car. Grabbing her coat and umbrella, she exited her vehicle. The clouds overhead looked threatening, as if it could rain buckets at any time, although occasional bursts of sunlight would penetrate the cloud's dark layers and shine forth in a warming radiance.

Barbara hurried to get inside, the wind gust impeding her progress with each step. Walking through the glass doors, she felt a pleasant blast of warm air.

Ahead of her, the sympathetic police sergeant, Bixby, sat at his desk. Walking up to the counter, Barbara asked to speak to Lieutenant Reed.

Bixby, familiar with her constant visits, responded, "Mrs. Harding, please have a seat on the bench, and I'll let the Lieutenant know you're here."

Bixby picked up the phone and dialed Reed's number. A minute later Barbara heard Bixby say, "Mrs. Harding's in the lobby wanting to see you."

Then the Sergeant responded, "I will do that; thank you, sir."

He hung up the phone and announced, "Mrs. Harding, go through the security doors, and have a seat inside. The lieutenant will call you shortly."

Barbara thanked him and entered the security area beyond the doors, sitting down on another worn, wooden bench as she observed the legal system in action. Here all social misfits ended their final days of freedom before being locked away for their crimes. Sadly, their victims, too, spent many hours here.

As Barbara looked around the busy office, she saw the different facets of police work. She watched the faces of some of the criminals being questioned by detectives, frightened at the way they looked back at her. Some of the people being questions seemed filled with despair; others only showed hatred and discontent.

Soon, however, she became impatient with waiting and wondered, *What is taking the lieutenant so long to call me?*

Finally, after more time had passed, Reed appeared and asked her to follow him back to his office. As she stood up, she glanced in the direction of a male gang member. Their eyes met. His look was pure, uninhibited hatred. A chill ran down her spine, and she thought, *I hope I never run into him in a dark alley*.

Her visits to the police station became a weekly occurrence, which the lieutenant would have to accept. Indeed, he must understand the frustration and pain both she and Mark had experienced. The only way to get answers was to visit police headquarters. Being a father himself, he would have to understand, she reasoned.

As she sat down in his office, Barbara began her usual interrogation. "Do you have any news on Melissa's abduction?"

Reed's response was always nearly the same. "No, we haven't heard anything new as of yet, but we're hopeful we'll hear something soon. You must never give up hope."

"Hope. That's all we have, and nothing else," Barbara announced, her frustration reaching new heights. She was tired of hearing the same thing.

Lieutenant Reed remained calm and stated the department's position in cases such as theirs. However, this time his remark was harsh and brutal to accept.

"I want you to realize, Mrs. Harding, there's little hope your daughter is still alive. I think it's time for you to accept the inevitable. I have to tell you the odds of her being alive are growing slimmer by the day."

Barbara refused to listen to this declaration of defeat by the White Plains Police Department. Jumping to her feet, she angrily addressed Reed. "As long as there's breath in my body, I will never stop searching for my daughter, Mr. Reed. If you don't like that, then I will complain to your captain that you're not doing your job!"

"Mrs. Harding, I didn't mean to upset you. I just thought you should understand when a child goes missing for a certain amount of time, seldom do they return."

Overcome with grief, Barbara fought back her emotions. "I'll go home, but you'll see me again—soon— whether you like it or not."

In a huff she picked up her purse and left. Scurrying through the busy office, she stopped at the security door and stood briefly, waiting to exit. No one paid her any attention except a young Hispanic male, who smiled devilishly back at her, seeing her pain.

Standing there waiting to be let out of the room, she felt naked and exposed to his eyes. The only thing she could do was repeatedly press the buzzer to get out. Finally, it went off, and she pressed her body against the heavy door, freeing herself from the confines of the secured area.

Chapter 6

As Barbara left the detectives' room, she passed by Sergeant Bixby without saying a word. Outside the rain had finally arrived in a steady downpour. The howling wind meant the deluge would continue for some time. Opening her umbrella, she ran to her car and, once inside, collapsed in an emotional flood of tears, pounding the steering wheel and shouting at the top of her lungs.

"How could Reed expect me to give up so easily? I will never stop looking for Melissa!"

Gripping the wheel until her knuckles turned white, Barbara felt a wave of white-hot anger. After several minutes of fuming, a strange calm engulfed her and a peculiar question, a feeling, popped into her head.

Could her daughter be somewhere close? Here, kept prisoner inside the city, imprisoned in any of these old buildings in White Plains. More times than she could count, it seemed as if Melissa's presence was calling out to her, wanting to be heard. Somehow as a mother, Barbara knew Melissa was still alive; she could feel a spiritual connection with her daughter that she couldn't explain.

Unexpectedly, Barbara's thoughts were interrupted by a gentle tapping on her window. Looking up, she noticed Sergeant Bixby standing under an umbrella. Surprised by his appearance, she quickly rolled down her car window and said, "Hello, can I help you?"

"Please listen. All of us at the station realize what you and your family have been going through. None of us could imagine losing a child, as you have done."

"No, I don't imagine none of you could,"

"Well, yes, okay. Listen, we just received word of a disturbance at the Rusty Anchor bar on Third Street. A customer there is causing a ruckus of sorts. According to the bartender, the man in question is Mark Harding."

"I know Bill, the bartender. He hosted our tenth wedding anniversary party some years back. They're not going to arrest Mark, are they?"

"No, of course not. The owner doesn't want to press charges, but I suggest you get there fast before your husband does something foolish."

"Great, what else could go wrong?"

"Don't fret yourself. Bill is a close friend of mine. He took a chance and called me at the station, searching for you. Otherwise, you would've found all sorts of messages on your answering machine."

"I cannot thank you enough, Sergeant. Listen, if it's not too much of an inconvenience, could you do me a favor and call my child's babysitter at home and tell her I have to stop by and pick up Mark on my way to their house?" Reaching into her purse, she took out a small piece of paper and scribbled a number down. Handing the paper to Bixby, she said, "The woman's name is Susan Bernstein."

"I know Susan Bernstein. She's quite the character, isn't she? You get going. I'll call and tell her you're running late."

"Thank you, again," Barbara responded.

Starting her car and leaving the station, she hurried to the Rusty Anchor to pick up Mark. On the way she thought about the inconvenience they were putting Susan through.

Barbara didn't like to impose on their friendship this

way. But now, what to do about Mark? He must know the strain all this put on her. Why now, with everything they'd been through, did he decide to get drunk? No, sir, she wouldn't let him get away from this without a lecture. If he were her child, a restriction would be in order. But she couldn't just tell Mark he must go to bed after supper; he'd laugh her to scorn—although making him feel guilty for his actions was always something she had stored in her arsenal.

At her interstate exit, she turned off and drove down Tyler Boulevard to Third Street, turned right, and continued for a quarter mile to the Rusty Anchor. Parking next to Mark's truck, she was relieved to discover he hadn't tried to drive home. Walking inside, she instantly recognized her husband sitting alone at the end of the bar, slumped over with a half-empty beer glass and six empty shot glasses beside him.

Barbara turned and looked at Bill, the bartender, who was drying beer mugs. She couldn't help but notice the disapproving look he gave Mark.

Walking up to the bar, Barbara apologized. "I was at the police station when Sergeant Bixby told me about Mark."

"Listen, Barb, I want you to know that it wasn't my idea that your husband got so tanked up. The truth is I tried to stop him from ordering extra shots, but you know Mark. He put up such a fight that it wasn't worth the hassle. Besides, I insisted he tell me where to find you before I would agree to pour him another drink—and he gave me his car keys. I felt confident he wasn't going anywhere."

"Again, I'm sorry, Bill. I'm not happy Mark is dealing with the loss of our daughter through alcohol."

"Everyone here understands. No worries."

Barbara approached Mark and, after taking a seat next to her husband, lovingly put her arm around his neck.

"Mark, honey, it's time to go home."

He drowsily looked up from the bar and greeted her in a slurred voice. "Hi there, cutie pie."

"Mark, what are you doing here? I thought you had a lodge meeting this evening,"

Mark turned to answer but instead tumbled off the barstool. Luckily, Barbara caught him before he fell to the floor. Using all her strength, she managed to push him back onto the stool. Looking past his silly grin, she stared directly into his eyes and said, "You're drunk!"

Thankfully, seeing Barbara with her hands full, a couple of the bar patrons came to her aid. Grabbing hold of Mark under his arms, they lifted him off the barstool and escorted him out of the bar toward Barbara's car.

They had only taken a few steps into the open air when Mark realized what was happening. He stood erect, pushed himself free from his supporters, stood up, and shouted, "I don't need anybody's damned help. I am just fine and can walk on my own."

As Mark stood there, his six-foot frame began swaying back and forth as he yelled, "I could kick all of your asses if I wanted! If you bastards want to help me, then tell me where I can find my little girl."

Without warning he broke down, crying like a small child. He stumbled forward and was about to fall to the ground when Barbara caught him.

The two guys standing by didn't dare approach Mark.

Barbara said plainly, "It's time to go."

Wrapping her left arm around his waist, she guided him to her car. Opening the passenger door, he fell into the seat, where he collapsed unconscious.

After thanking the men, she quickly got into her car and drove to Susan's house to pick up Rachel. While on the way, she angrily expressed her desire for Mark to get therapy. Yes, he was snoring and wouldn't hear her. Still, it helped her ease her anger toward her husband. She was growing tired of his failed attempts to deal with matters through alcohol. After tonight's little fiasco, Barbara would make her point known, whether he liked it or not.

She discussed her feelings about the abduction while Mark lay there, oblivious to the world around him, only responding with a moan or grunt. Thinking of his performance in the bar, she became more upset by the moment.

She wasn't about to allow Mark's selfish attitude to continue without being challenged. *He needs to know she's not going to lose the love of her life because of Melissa's disappearance.* Neither was she going to chock this up to being just another tragedy that families faced and broke apart over because they couldn't handle the stress.

By the time Barbara pulled into the driveway of the Bernsteins' house, dusk had fallen. Mark hadn't moved from his resting spot and had begun to snore louder than before. Suddenly, she was furious with him; he hadn't heard a word she had said. She slammed the car door and left him to sleep it off while she went inside to pick up Rachel.

Susan met her at the door and said, "I see you found Mark."

"Yes, he was at the Rusty Anchor bar, getting smashed."

"I've already taken the liberty of feeding Rachel," Susan explained.

Barbara thanked her for the help and added, "I don't know what I would've done without you. Where is Rachel?" she asked, looking around.

"Oh, she's in the den with John; he's helping her with her math homework. Why don't you come inside the house? I'm sure Mark won't mind."

Barbara turned around and looked back in the direction

of the car. Seeing no sign of life, she agreed to Susan's invitation and followed her into the house. They continued into the den, where Rachel and John were intently discussing a math problem.

Barbara silently watched Rachel agonize over the math problem, making tiny scribbles on a piece of paper as John looked on patiently. After a few intense moments working on the problem, Rachel came up with the correct answer and wrote it down.

John smiled and announced loudly, "That's correct! The problem is solved."

Ecstatic, Rachel jumped up and gave a loving hug to her tutor.

John was thrilled and reminded Rachel she could do better in school if she concentrated more on what her teacher was teaching her instead of watching cartoons on the television.

Rachel responded, "I like cartoons! They're fun to watch."

"I know," John replied, "but knowledge is to be treasured over cartoons, especially if you want a career as a doctor or scientist."

Barbara spoke up from across the room, agreeing with John, and then told Rachel it was time to go. Rachel slammed her math book shut and tucked it into her backpack. She greeted her mother with a big hug and stood next to her, ready to go.

Turning to leave, Barb thanked Susan and John for their hospitality, saying, "Tomorrow will be different; I won't be so late, I promise."

"Don't give it another thought. Please drive safely," Susan said.

A final hug later, both Rachel and Barbara got into the car. When Rachel opened the passenger door, she saw her father sleeping in the front seat. Closing the door, she opened the rear door instead and clambered inside, accidentally whacking her dad in the head with her heavy backpack.

To her surprise it didn't faze him in the least. She had only seen him like this one other time when he was sick for days and could do nothing but sleep; however, this was different. He gave off a sickening smell that filled the car, almost making her sick to her stomach. The driver's door opened; her mother got inside and drove home. On their way Barbara questioned Rachel about school.

"Oh, school's okay, Mom. Everyone treats me with kindness since Melissa went away."

"I'm glad to hear that," Barbara responded. "Some kids can be cruel when they see families going through difficult times. They can say mean things, not realizing what they're saying. So what did you study today?"

"We studied character assassination and diversity in our humanities class," Rachel announced.

"Oh, that's nice," Barbara replied, somewhat distracted by the sounds of Mark's loud snoring.

Rachel then explained she had learned a valuable truth in life and said, "Honesty is better than lying; if you are always honest, it will prevent you from having problems in your future."

"That's right, honey. Your father and I have always taught you and your sister to be honest because if you lie, I'll know it," Barbara proclaimed.

"I haven't lied, Mom," Rachel responded, "except I didn't say anything, either."

"What are you saying, Rachel?"

After a moment of silence Rachel spoke up, "The other day I overheard someone at school bragging that they knew who took Melissa." Rachel began crying.

Barbara slammed on the brakes, bringing the car to a

screeching stop. Mark, still snoozing, slammed against the dashboard. Luckily, at that time of night the roadway was lightly traveled. Roused from his stupor, Mark yelled at Barbara about her lack of driving skills but remained half unconscious, briefly rubbing his sore head, and unaware of where he was so he went back to sleep.

Barbara paid him no attention; instead, she turned toward the backseat and excitedly grabbed Rachel by her arms. "What secrets have you been keeping from me, Rachel?"

Once more roused from his slumber, Mark wondered what the hell was happening around him. He regained enough of his senses to see his wife shaking Rachel angrily from the driver's seat as she continued her interrogation, with Rachel crying, "Mom, you're hurting her arms."

"You better tell me everything you know this instant child, or so help me!"

"Mom, it was a girl at school named Jessica Taylor! She's the one who told everyone at school that she saw some men dressed in black kidnap Melissa."

"What men?" Barbara shouted.

"People that drove a blue van and wore a hooded cover over their heads," Rachel responded.

"A blue van," Barbara repeated.

"That's what Jessica was saying. I asked her if she saw the men that kidnapped Melissa, and she said, yes, she did."

"Tell me again what this Jessica was telling your friends at school," Barbara asked frantically, not believing what she had heard.

"Jessica told me she saw some guys grab Melissa and throw her in a van. The man driving the van told Jessica that they would come to her house and kill all of her family if she told anyone about what she saw. Mom, I was scared. I didn't know what to do. That's why I never said anything. I don't want them to go to Jessica's house and kill her family!"

Barbara shoved her car into gear and drove madly to a convenience store. Coming to a squealing stop in front of two payphones, she grabbed her change purse and leaped from her car. Standing in front of the payphones, she quickly inserted a coin into the pay slot and dialed Detective Reed's phone number. After a couple of rings, she heard Reed's voice on the other end of the phone.

Barbara excitedly shouted, "Detective Reed! I just found out some information on Melissa's abductors. Can we meet this evening sometime?"

"Sorry, I can't see you tonight. I'm late for a meeting." He suggested they meet tomorrow afternoon, promising to take her statement then.

Disappointed, Barbara hung up and returned to her car. In the back seat Rachel continued sobbing while Mark was coming to, rubbing his aching head, trying to make sense of what had just happened. No one spoke. Barbara was upset at Reed's lack of enthusiasm, especially after hearing about a possible break in the case; she held her anger the rest of the way home.

That night, too upset to talk to anyone, Barbara stayed up while Mark and Rachel went to bed. She busied herself with cleaning the kitchen until she couldn't resist the effects of sleeplessness any longer. Arriving in their bedroom, Barbara got into bed and pulled the sheets up around her head. Quickly falling to sleep, she wanted nothing more than to see this day come to an end.

Chapter 7

The following day the annoying alarm clock woke Mark from his sleep. Rolling over, he noticed Barbara was up taking her shower. Images of his time at the bar flashed into his memory. Simultaneously, he felt a sharp pain pounding in his head. He had made a big mistake by getting so drunk; he knew he was going to catch hell for it. Reluctantly crawling out of bed, he went into the steamy bathroom.

"You're up awfully early," he announced over the sound of the rushing water.

"After hearing Rachel's story that someone at her school saw Melissa's kidnappers, I couldn't sleep a wink and thought it best to get up and start the day. I'm surprised you could drag your drunken ass out of bed after the amount of booze you had last night," Barbara responded sarcastically.

"About that—" Mark replied, intending to explain.

Barbara chose not to hear whatever fanciful excuse he had for getting drunk and cut him off before he could say another word. "After work today I'm going to the police station to meet with Detective Reed."

"I don't think knowing the type of vehicle that took Melissa is going to change anything," Mark responded.

"Oh, really?" Barbara retorted. "I didn't expect you heard any part of the conversation Rachel and I had last night. You were so damn drunk. I'm surprised you remember anything all. Do you remember picking a fight with the two guys who were helping me carry you to the car? Do you remember that?"

Opening the shower curtain, Barbara popped her head out and asked pointedly, "What the hell is your problem, Mark?"

"I feel it's a waste of time."

"Oh no, Mark. There's something more you're not telling me," Barbara responded.

Shutting off the water and reaching for her towel, she wrapped it around her wet body. Stepping out of the shower, she grabbed hold of another towel and twisted it around her head.

Mark stared at his reflection in the mirror, unsure how to respond. He needed to choose his words wisely; he knew he'd drank too much. His head was pounding as though someone hit him with a hammer. Putting last night's blunders aside, he said. "I never really told you about the way I feel about Melissa's disappearance."

Removing the towel on her head, Barbara began to brush out her hair as she listened intently to Mark's explanation. Although she was still angry with him because of last night's fiasco, for now, she chose to put it behind her. Never to be forgotten, it would always be remembered.

Mark paused, briefly searching for the words to describe his feelings. Finally, he blurted out, "A girl Melissa's age doesn't stand a chance in a world like today." Then, unexpectedly, he admitted something he had kept hidden from her the entire time. Somberly, he declared, "I doubt Melissa is alive."

"How can you say that?" Barbara cried out angrily.

"Because I have faced the facts and come to terms with it! Making stupid posters and hanging them on telephone poles across town isn't going to bring Melissa back, no matter how hard you try. Whoever has taken her has, no doubt, raped her, repeatedly, and discarded her body along the road somewhere."

"You are a real bastard at times!" Barbara screamed. "How could you give up so quickly? I don't understand you; you've changed so much. You're an entirely different person than the man I married. I don't know you anymore!"

Mark retained his composure in the face of his wife's anguish and tried his best to explain his reasoning. "I have learned to accept the inevitable." He turned and walked out of the bathroom, slamming the door behind him.

Barbara realized she was utterly alone to face the challenge of finding Melissa—apparently, without any support from the man she loved.

She felt betrayed and desperate; she had no tears to cry. Instead, she became even more determined to prove Mark wrong. She knew Melissa was still alive; she felt it deep in her soul, as only a mother could.

Mark had said some hurtful things, and when she appeared in the kitchen, she didn't engage in conversation with him but made herself some breakfast and told Rachel to hurry up and finish her cereal before they were late getting her to school.

Once Rachel was ready, Barbara walked her out to the curb and waited for the bus to arrive. Soon the yellow bus appeared, and after Rachel was safely aboard, Barbara returned to the house and silently grabbed her purse and car keys. After opening the garage door, she got inside her vehicle and started the engine. As she was driving away, Mark was left behind to start his day. Alone.

Barbara made her way to work and prepared herself for another uneventful day. Once inside the large building, she rode the crowded elevator to the fifth floor. After stopping several times on each ascending level to allow people to exit, she eventually arrived at work. Once inside both receptionists wished her a pleasant morning; afterward, arriving at her desk, Barbara removed her coat and placed it around her chair. After setting her purse down into her desk drawer, she walked to the break room for a morning cup of coffee, thinking about what Mark had said about Melissa.

While she stood next to the sink, stirring in the creamer, one of the company's bookkeepers, Brenda Hawking, entered the room.

"Good morning, Barbara. How you've been, girl?"

"Hey, Brenda, I'm okay, considering. How are things in bookkeeping?"

"Oh, you know how it is. You're the little mouse people never notice, that is, until you leave a little mouse turd on the counter. Then everyone freaks out and calls an exterminator."

Barbara laughed at Brenda's candor and took another sip of her coffee, thinking it felt good to laugh again. Brenda asked her if she had heard any more news from the police about her missing daughter.

"No, we haven't heard anything yet, but we're hopeful the police will hear something soon," Barbara replied.

"Well, everyone here is praying for your daughter's safe return."

"Our family appreciates that," Barbara answered.

Mr. Bennet, Barbara's director, unexpectedly walked into the kitchen with his empty coffee cup and said, "Barbara, I'm glad to see you. Tell me, any news on your missing daughter?"

"No, I'm afraid not,"

"That's truly regrettable. I'm so sorry to hear that."

"Yes, all we can do is hope and pray she comes home soon."

Unexpectedly, a group of young executives from advertising burst into the small space, laughing and joking about whose favorite baseball team won, shattering the somber mood over the weekend.

Mr. Bennet, excusing himself, leaned forward between the two women and filled his coffee cup. Afterward, he turned toward Barbara and said, "There's something we need to discuss, perhaps sometime this morning. I'll call you and let you know."

She acknowledged his request with a simple nod and left the breakroom. Returning to her desk, she went to work on one of the numerous projects that needed updating, the entire time thinking to herself, *It's rarely a good thing when your boss tells you there needs to be a chat.*

Chapter 8

Barbara prepared herself for the worst. She realized she'd missed a lot of work while dealing with Melissa's disappearance. She tried not to imagine the worst, but the truth was, getting called into your manager's office for a conversation was scary, something she wished to avoid. There was talk of trimming the corporate fat. Every department had a new set of guidelines with the explicit goal to streamline business. There were layoffs involved in the process.

Anticipating Mr. Bennet's call, Barbara's stomach turned upside down as nervousness flooded her while pondering the question: *What possible reason could he have for wanting to see me?*

Just then, her telephone rang. Mr. Bennet asked her to come up to his office; there was a personal matter he wanted to discuss with her. When she hung up the phone and stood to leave, her legs felt wobbly as she walked down the long hallway toward his office. Knocking on his door, she heard his voice say, "Come in."

She opened the door and stepped inside, advancing slowly and apprehensively. Mr. Bennet sat behind a dark mahogany desk, reviewing some paperwork. Looking up briefly, he motioned for her to have a seat.

He stared directly at Barbara and announced, "It has

come to the attention of the firm that you have been preoccupied lately with problems at home. As a result, you have lost a lot of time at work,"

"Yes, I realize that. But I'm working toward resolving my problems at home. Please, believe me, it's just been a little bit harder than I expected, Mr. Bennet!" she responded and began making excuses for the days missed from her job. "I know I've been slipping up," Barbara explained, feeling uncomfortable and leaning forward in her seat to address her boss more personally. "I'll try to do better."

Feeling overwhelmed, she began to weep, her mascara running down her cheeks. She pleaded with quivering lips not to be fired. Nothing to lose, Barbara implored her boss for another chance, promising she would do better at her job.

"Barbara! You're not going to lose your job! The opposite is true. Please allow me to explain. I've recently talked it over with the CEO of the company, and we've decided to give you two months' leave to get your affairs in order—with pay, of course."

Barbara stared at Mr. Bennet in astonishment, not sure how to react.

"We're doing this because you're a valuable asset to the firm. We want you to take this time off so you can get your head straight. Think of it as a hiatus."

Barbara sat, speechless, her mouth dropping to the floor in awkward silence. "I don't know what to say."

"That's okay. You don't have to say a word," Mr. Bennet responded. "We're having a girl from a temp agency drop by; she'll assume your duties at the firm until you return. Barbara, take this girl under your wing. Show her around the office for the rest of the day. Let her see how you handle your job and, if need be, we always have Erma, the office manager, to help if she runs into any snags. Today will be your last day here at work for now. We won't be seeing you back here until the beginning of next year."

The blank look on Barbara's face said it all. She tried to respond but couldn't find the words to express her gratitude. Instead, she nodded her head in agreement but remained speechless.

Mr. Bennet stood, walked around his desk, and gave her a friendly handshake, reassuring her that her job would be there when she returned. Then he looked at her directly and said, "I want to see the old Barbara return, the one that we all know and love."

"Yes, Mr. Bennet, I want that with my whole being! To have our lives return to ordinary before my daughter went missing, I would never want for anything ever again, believe me."

"Now we have some work to do. Let's get to it."

Mr. Bennet guided Barbara to the door. In the hallway she stood silently, trying to digest what had just happened. She felt both numb and exhilarated.

When she reached her desk and sat down, Barbara froze in place, taking a moment to contemplate what Mr. Bennet had said, slowly grasping the opportunity that had presented itself. Freedom for the next two months to focus on finding Melissa.

The pink sticky note on her calendar announced the ten o'clock budget meeting. Already regretting the commitment, she took a pen and notebook and headed to the breakroom to top off her coffee cup before the meeting. A line of employees was already heading the same way, and none seemed eager to attend the meeting. Resigned, she found a seat next to Peggy, a new hire in Human Resources and someone Barb had liked from the moment they'd met.

Peggy leaned closer and whispered, "Congratulations are in order, I take it!"

Surprised, Barbara turned to examine her friend and

said, "What do you mean?"

"I cannot go into detail right now but listen, who do you suppose drew up the Leave of Absence paperwork? Yours truly," Peggy laughed.

"Well, thanks a lot. The least you could have done was give me a fair warning. I was terrified."

"Oh no, I had strict orders to keep it hush, hush. If I had told you and Mr. Bennet saw you weren't shocked, he would have guessed someone had spilled the beans, and my goose would have been cooked, for sure," Peggy laughed. "Hey, regardless, look at what you're getting, an all-expenses-paid vacation!"

Seeing the look on Barbara's face, Peggy realized how silly she sounded. She backpeddled and said, "Oh, never mind, that was stupid of me. I'm so sorry. I pray I never have to face what your family is experiencing, no matter how much time they gave me off from work. That was stupid; I'm sorry." Peggy grabbed Barbara's hand.

"I wouldn't wish this on my most hated enemy," Barbara announced.

A female voice broke the awkward silence. "Hello, everyone. Thank you for coming."

The rest of that morning's meeting was a blur. Barbara scribbled down thoughts onto paper and outlined details of her plan to find Melissa. A great place to start would be to meet with Reed that afternoon. After all, she had news to tell him about the possible getaway vehicle used in the kidnapping.

Next she thought of Susan's suggestion and wrote down "Sterling" and a question mark. Then she jotted down "Jessica Taylor" and started to add another question mark. Still, as she bore down on the paper until her pencil punched through the other side, she thought, *Yet to be discovered your reason for announcing to your classmates that you saw*

Melissa's kidnappers. Why would you say such a thing unless it was to get at Rachel? Perhaps it's nothing more than a childhood rivalry?

Distracting her from her thoughts, Barbara heard a male voice say, "I thank you all for coming. Don't forget to fill out your survey cards and drop them in the suggestion box before you go home this afternoon."

"I'm glad that's over with," Peggy announced.

"Yes. Me, too," Barbara answered.

"Look, I feel terrible about what I said or didn't say. I was insensitive. I just want you to know that."

"For what? Forget it. I have."

"Shit! There I go again, being insensitive," Peggy apologized.

"All right, listen, it's time to get back to work, the real work that keeps this company afloat. I should go."

"Barb, please promise me you'll say goodbye before you leave, all right?"

"Yes, no problem. I'll see you soon,"

Getting back to work, Barbara knew she still had things to accomplish before leaving for the day. She began closing old accounts and filing them away in their proper place inside the greyish metal cabinet. Sometime later, while she was updating a file, Mr. Bennet appeared with a young girl who looked to be in her early twenties.

"Barbara, do you have a moment?"

"Yes, certainly."

"I'd like to introduce you to Latoya. She's the temp who is here to assume your duties while you're away."

Leaning forward to shake the girl's hand, Barbara welcomed her to the firm. Barbara spent the rest of the day teaching Latoya the various facets of her job. The end of the day came quicker than expected, and soon Barbara was locking her desk and preparing to leave.

However, keeping a promise made, she stopped by the fourth floor to tell Peggy goodbye but couldn't find her in the maze of cubicle offices in the H.R. department. Marsha, another H.R staff person who Barbara met some years ago during a fundraiser, walked by.

"Excuse me, Marsha, could you tell me if you've seen Peggy around?"

"Yes. Well, I overheard her on the phone talking with the school. Her son Richard got into a fight, and she had to leave work,"

"All right, could you tell her for me that I stopped by?"

"Certainly, Barbara, please listen for a moment before you go. Everyone in Human Resources thinks it's fantastic that the company is willing to give you a leave of absence to search for your daughter. It says something about your work performance."

"I feel grateful to be working for a great boss; otherwise, who knows if I'd still have a job."

"Being a mother myself, I want to wish you all the best."

"Thank you. Please excuse me; I have to run."

"Take care. Please keep us posted on anything new about your daughter."

"I will. Thank you again, bye."

Leaving the building, Barbara stopped briefly before getting into her car. She stared up at the fifth floor and thought of all the close friends she's made over the years. Everyone was supportive of her plight. The most sympathetic was Mr. Bennet. A father of four children, he plainly understood the difficulties of losing a child, especially since losing his eldest son to a boating accident.

"I will miss you all," she whispered, then got in her car and drove away.

Chapter 9

Arriving at the police station, Barbara walked up to the sergeant's desk to check in and surprisingly got buzzed through without delay. Detective Reed quickly led her to his office. As soon as Barbara sat down, she excitedly described what she had heard from Rachel concerning Jessica Taylor.

Reed jotted down everything on a piece of paper. When Barbara had finished giving the details, the lieutenant assured her that he would investigate this new evidence, promising to meet with the Taylor girl and her family very soon.

Leaving the station, Barbara returned to her car and drove away. On the way to the Bernsteins', she felt optimistic that these latest details would lead to Melissa's whereabouts. When she pulled into the driveway, Susan's car was missing. Walking up to the door and gently knocking, she was greeted by John.

"Please, come inside."

"Where's Susan?"

"Oh, she had to go to the store for some milk. I'm glad we have a moment alone. There's something I want to discuss with you."

"Okay, what is it, John?"

"Well," he began.

Then Rachel appeared wearing her backpack and said,

"I'm ready to go!"

"Okay, honey, go wait for me in the car. I'll be along in a minute," Barbara replied.

"All right, whatever you say," Rachel answered.

"I'm sorry, John. Please continue with what you were saying."

"Barbara, I've been thinking about Melissa a lot lately. This morning an idea came to me. I remember meeting a detective at the White Plains Police Department several years ago named Jack Danbury."

"Yes! What about him?" Barbara responded.

"Well, he has a friend who has some connection with the supernatural, and I think he might be able to help find Melissa."

"What makes you think his friend will help me?" she asked.

"I don't know that he will," he replied. "He's a strange duck, if you ask me; I only met him once some time back while working a case involving a missing child. He was able to help us quite a bit. He even told us where to look for the body; he somehow knew where it was located."

"The body? John, so what you're telling me is he couldn't save the child?"

"I'm afraid no one could save that kid. But listen to me, Jack is his only real friend in this world. If you can persuade Jack to help you, then perhaps you'll get his psychic friend to find Melissa."

"Thank you, John, but I just left the police station a short time ago. However, if you feel it will make a difference, I'll return to convince this Jack Danbury to help me."

"I believe he'll be a great help, Barb," John replied.

"John, what did you say his name was?"

"Who, Jack?"

"No, the supernatural guy."

"He goes by the name of Sterling. Not Mr. Sterling or Fred Sterling or anything like that, just Sterling!"

"All right, I have got to go. Rachel's waiting in the car."

"Do you want me to say anything to Susan?"

"Yes, tell her I'll give her a call sometime tomorrow."

"You got it. Take care, and be safe driving home," John replied.

Hurrying to her car, Barbara drove off. While Rachel sat quietly listening to her Walkman. Barbara had time to think. *This is the second time I've heard that name Sterling; I can't help but wonder if he's genuinely a psychic with mystical powers to find missing persons. I never considered using the help of a psychic before. It's intriguing. It's something else to consider; perhaps I'll find myself traveling upon a new path in life, even if I'm not sure where it will take me. Finding a body—I don't care for the sound of that.*

When she arrived home and started dinner, she felt exhausted. Hamburger Helper was the quickest and least-complained-about meal. She quickly opened a pound of hamburger and began cooking it in the skillet when a panicked-looking Rachel appeared in the kitchen.

"Mom, you have to come quick! I thought I saw someone looking at me through my window."

"What! Show me. Now."

Racing through the house, Barbara headed down the hallway toward Rachel's bedroom. When she arrived and looked inside, nothing seemed out of the ordinary; her L.P. had finished playing and traveled back and forth at the end of the record. Other than that, everything seemed normal. By normal, it looked like a complete mess. Clothes were scattered about; her trash can was filled to overflowing.

Stepping over to the window, Barbara looked outside into the darkness of the backyard. Seeing Mark busy in the garage, she turned to Rachel and said, "It must have been your father. I see he just got home; that's all it was. Nothing to be worried about."

But just as she turned to leave, she experienced another strange phenomenon. In front of her a transparent pocket of air felt frigid to the touch. *Okay*, she thought, *what is this?*

Bravely ignoring her intuition and common sense, she walked into the unknown and felt a weird sensation. *Strange, strange indeed.* Turning back, she saw Rachel, standing and looking at her strangely. She called out, but it was inaudible; her words were muffled as if underwater. Suddenly, she heard a voice—not Rachel's. It came from a great distance, saying words she couldn't understand—all except one, in particular, that rang out like a bell: "Bishop"—her last name.

Barbara grabbed Rachel and ran from the room. Stopping in the kitchen, they paused briefly while catching their breaths.

"Mom, what is it?" Rachel screamed.

"Nothing. Rachel, it's fine. I thought I saw a spider. That's all so nothing to worry about."

"Mom, are you okay? You're really scaring me!"

Mark appeared in the kitchen and said, "Something smells good." He was oblivious to the strange occurrence in Rachel's bedroom and went into the refrigerator to get a beer.

"Shoot! The dinner is burning!" Racing to the stove, Barbara turned it off.

"Hey Hon, don't worry about it. Let's go out and get a pizza instead."

"I guess, why not? Mark, please listen to me for once, okay? There's something we need to talk about."

"It seems lately there's always something we need to talk about. Why should tonight be any different?" Mark complained.

"Mark, please listen to me. Strange things have been

happening around here. But besides this, I want to tell you about what happened today at my work."

"Listen, Barb, come on. Let's go get a pizza. I don't complain to you about my job."

"Damn it, listen to me for just one minute, will you? I'm not complaining about my job. I just want to let you know my firm gave me a leave of absence so I could concentrate on finding Melissa."

"I hope your leave was with pay; I mean, there's talk at the plant of layoffs. I can't afford to pay for everything, you know."

"Let's just go get a pizza," Barbara surrendered.

"Sure, I'll drive." Opening the refrigerator door, Mark returned his beer to the metal rack and told it, "I won't be enjoying you tonight after all."

Inside the family car Barbara sat feeling disappointed by her husband's reaction. She felt alone in her quest to find their daughter. Admittedly, it wasn't all his fault; Mark had tried his best to search for Melissa but soon ran out of steam.

Barbara would get her point across, she thought. Sometime that night she would ease Mark's worries by telling him that her leave was with pay. But when it comes to telling him of the strange experiences she'd had in their house, she preferred to keep that to herself. The support from her spouse was nonexistent, but she wouldn't be deterred. She knew she was in for a fight—but who was her adversary?

Chapter 10

On Wednesday morning the sun rays teemed through Barbara's bedroom window. She appreciated the extra sleep she was afforded by not having to go to work. Still, she had a schedule to maintain. Mark had already gotten up and left; she could smell the strong odor of brewed coffee permeating the house. He had begun working overtime as his way of contributing to the family's needs while she started her hiatus.

When she had explained to her husband that Mr. Bennet had arranged for her to stay home for the next two months, Mark had been surprised, especially the part about how she would still be paid.

When Rachel awoke the smell coming from the kitchen was inviting. She thought it odd that her mother would be cooking breakfast, particularly on a school day. Regardless, she excitedly left her bedroom and appeared in the kitchen.

"Good morning, Mom. What's for breakfast?"

"I'm making your favorite: pancakes, bacon, and eggs."

"Awesome, goodness," Rachel replied.

After breakfast while Barbara drove her daughter to school and listened intently to her daughter describe her typical day at school, she was surprised to hear that Rachel wanted to play a musical instrument. Typical for her age, she was absorbed in who she liked and didn't like in school. When it came to her studies, she freely admitted her problems with math.

Barbara listened and offered encouragement. "If we need to get you a tutor, we can certainly arrange that for you."

She pulled up to the school and got in line. Finally, when Barbara's turn came, Rachel grabbed her heavy backpack and opened the door. She started to step outside but paused as if she had forgotten something. Unexpectedly, she turned around, wrapped her arms around her mother's neck, and said, "I love you, Mom." Then she jumped out of the car and ran toward her classroom.

Barbara didn't move until the driver behind her honked. Driving away, she whispered, "I love you, too, honey." She felt deeply touched by her daughter's simple gesture.

When she arrived at the police station, finding a parking space was naturally a chore. After circling in and out of the lot for several minutes, she finally saw someone leaving near the front of the building and eagerly took that space. After parking she had a short walk to reach the front door.

Inside she approached a new desk sergeant, whom she had never met, and asked to see Lieutenant Reed. Then she sat down and waited, gratefully thinking at least this wasn't the Department of Motor Vehicles; otherwise, she'd have to wait for hours.

It wasn't long before the sergeant called her name and, with a press of the buzzer, Barbara passed through the security door into the detectives' area. She took a seat on the now-familiar solid bench and waited patiently for Reed.

Until that day she hadn't surveyed her surroundings. However, with nothing but time on her hands, she looked around the room, ignoring the criminals within. Many pictures and certificates were proudly displayed on the walls, boasting of the detectives' various achievements while working at the station.

On the wall above her was a newspaper article she found most interesting. It showed Detective Jack Danbury shaking hands with the mayor. The caption read: "Detective from White Plains, New York, solves child abduction case."

Unfortunately, the article announced the child was found dead, murdered by a child stalker. The man, named Felix, had been set free from prison because of overcrowding, slipping between the judicial system's cracks.

He was now awaiting his execution on death row. *I wonder if that's the story John told me about,* Barbara thought. Near that picture was another photo showing Jack Danbury receiving a medal of valor for saving his partner's life in a shoot-out; he'd been wounded as a result. He wore a sling across his chest where the bullet had entered his body, exiting his back.

Just then she overheard some commotion from across the room. She turned around and saw Detective Danbury talking to a younger-looking detective he addressed as Frank.

Danbury was somewhat overweight and appeared to be in his mid to late fifties. He had thin gray hair and a thick mustache. At the moment he was joyfully amused by his partner's reaction to losing a bet they had made on a football team.

Frank snapped, "You wouldn't have won the bet at all if you hadn't gotten help from that psychic friend of yours."

The argument was abruptly interrupted by the sound of a ringing phone on the younger detective's desk. As he reached for the phone, he pointed his finger at his partner and told Jack that he would continue their conversation over lunch.

"Sure thing, since you're the one who's buying it," Jack responded, laughing loudly.

Frank answered his phone and said, "Detective Richards, can I help you?"

As he listened to the caller, he sat down at his desk and began writing something on a pad of paper. Barbara's interest was more focused on Jack, the other detective, who had just sat down at his desk and started to review some files. She remained curious about the psychic friend he knew. As she studied Jack carefully, she waited for an opportunity to speak to him. Getting up her nerve, Barbara approached him as he was preoccupied with a criminal file.

"Excuse me, Detective Danbury," Barbara said. "I couldn't help but overhear you talking with the other detective about the use of your friend's psychic abilities to help you win the bet."

Jack didn't bother to look up from his paperwork and responded, "Yes, what about it?"

"My name is Barbara. I'm the mother of Melissa Harding, the young girl gone missing about three weeks ago. I believe your psychic friend helped you solve a case that was similar to mine—"

Jack cut her off before she could say another word. "Wait a cotton-picking minute, lady. What do you think this is anyway—a psychic hotline?"

"Heavens, no," Barbara responded apologetically. "I just thought if I could talk to your psychic friend about Melissa's abduction, I'm sure he would be willing to help me."

Jack's anger began to burn, and he looked up at Barbara and said bluntly, "Honestly, I don't have time to call my friend and ask if he'd help you find your kid. I'm a very busy man at the moment. I'd appreciate it if you would walk away and leave me alone."

"Please listen. My daughter could be suffering and close to death—taken by some madman! And all you can do is worry about your stupid paperwork?"

"Ma'am, I'm not sure why you're bothering me, but I'm examining criminal files, and you are obstructing my investigation. If you don't cease annoying me, I'll have to arrest you," Jack calmly answered.

Barbara was surprised by the detective's statement and began shouting back in response, "That's all I need right now is to be arrested for bothering an officer of the law!" She shook her head in disgust, turned away, and began to cry.

Jack tried to ignore the woman's sobbing, but he knew he wasn't going to get any work done with this lady bawling her eyes out in front of him. In haste he said, "Lady cut off the waterworks. I'm not buying the sad mother routine."

Jack's response only upset Barbara more; she cried louder. Turning back to confront the detective, she proclaimed, "Melissa was taken from a caring home where both her parents loved her deeply." She continued to weep.

Overwhelmed by Barbara's tears, Jack finally, reluctantly, agreed to give his friend a call. But before he did, he made Barbara promise to leave him alone.

"If Sterling chooses not to help you, that's the end of it. You won't bother me again."

Barbara nodded in agreement as she dug in her purse for a tissue to wipe away her tears and running mascara.

Jack reached into his wallet and pulled out a business card. Written on the back in red ink was a phone number. Looking down, Barbara quickly memorized the phone number. A feeling of anticipation gripped her. With luck this psychic would help her— especially if he understood how desperate she was to find Melissa, the man wouldn't be able to resist helping her.

She stood near Jack's desk, drying her eyes and listening intently as the phone rang with no answer. Suddenly, a man's faint voice on the other end of the receiver said, "Hello?"

Jack apologetically responded, "It's me, Danbury. Listen, I have this lady standing next to me. Ah, hell—have you heard of the Harding case?" Jack waited in silence for a response, as did Barbara, listening anxiously.

A faint masculine whisper said, "Yes, I'm familiar with the case."

"Well, the missing girl's mother wants your help, solving it."

After another brief silence, the man said, "Jack, last time we spoke I told you I couldn't be distracted; I'm working on another missing child case."

"Yes, I know," Jack answered. "But this Barbara Harding is persistent, and she started to cry! You know how I can't stand to see a female crying."

Regardless of Jack's protest, Barbara listened to Danbury's next series of grunts and groans, doing his best to express regret to his friend for the interruption. This Sterling seemed upset. Barbara didn't care. Over the past few weeks the dull, predictable, shy woman had faded away, and in her place was a tough, hardened, outspoken mama who didn't care about formalities and was driven to find her missing daughter. People's bruised feelings were a nicety she could no longer afford.

When Jack got off the phone, he said to her, "Sterling can't help you. I did all I could do. So now, could you please leave me alone?"

Barbara nodded in agreement and said, "Thanks for trying, Detective Danbury. Could you please tell the desk sergeant I'm ready to leave?"

"I'm sorry, I tried. Give me a moment, and I'll call up front."

Back in the front lobby, she informed the desk sergeant that she wasn't going to wait to see Lieutenant Reed.

"I'll make it another time," she announced and walked out of the police station, angry and upset.

Chapter II

Jack had no way of knowing Barbara had memorized the phone number he just dialed. After she left the station she searched her purse for a piece of paper to write it down before she forgot it. She chuckled at the thought that she'd been able to outfox the detective. For now she would gladly pay all she possessed to have that phone number.

Stealing the phone was nothing more than a desperate move by a needy mother. *Damn the police*, she thought. *They should realize how frantic I am. Besides, there's no law against memorizing a phone number.*

Now that she had Sterling's number, she wasn't the least bit timid about calling. But what should she say? Placing this phone call would require finesse; she didn't have time to explain herself. Sterling might hang up without even listening; how could she explain her desperation?

Once home she intended to dial the number. Why put it off? Every hour wasted is less time Melissa has to stay alive. First, she let out the dog, Buster, and walked out to her garden to check on her roses. As she deadheaded the old buds, she heard the phone ringing inside the kitchen. Frantically running to answer it, she gasped, "Hello?"

Lieutenant Reed answered, "Mrs. Harding, what happened? The desk sergeant informed me that you dropped by the station to speak to me. When I came out, you were gone."

"Yes, um, please forgive me, Detective," Barbara replied. "Something happened at home, you understand?"

"Oh, yes, being a parent with two sons still in school, I get it. Perhaps we could meet next week. How does that sound?"

"Sure, that'll be okay. What about Tuesday, the eleventh, say around ten o'clock?" she quickly answered.

"Great. I have it marked down on the calendar; I'll see you then."

"Thank you and goodbye, Detective," Barbara responded.

After hanging up the phone she decided talking to the police was just a waste of time. After all, Mark had already given up on them; why shouldn't she? Still, she didn't want to burn any bridges. There was a slim chance the police could find Melissa alive and well.

She just wanted it all to be over. She could never accept that Melissa was dead. She focused instead on her being alive somewhere and, most importantly, that she wasn't in any pain or suffering. She hoped all of this would soon come to an end.

Walking in the pantry, she got herself a package of HoHos and ripped it open. While she munched on the snack, she thought of the scratch paper containing the psychic's number inside her purse.

Even though she had written it down on paper, the number was etched in her memory. She drew a breath, searching for the courage to call Sterling, not knowing the outcome of such an intrusion into his mysterious world. She was, after all, the invader who could find herself repelled by all the energy he had at his disposal, but she didn't care. What's the worst the guy can do? Hang up on me? She giggled.

Determined to get it over with, she returned to her purse and took out the small piece of paper. *Fate will have a hand in the outcome,* she thought. What harm can there be if I dialed the number? What should she say? What if she had to explain how she'd gotten his number?

She picked up the receiver and heard the dial tone hum. She looked at the number once again and, with shaking, nervous fingers, punched the numbers on the phone. When she pressed the last one, the phone began ringing. For a split second she almost hung up, but she quickly abandoned that idea as she thought of her daughter being tortured, unable to find help.

A man's voice said, "Hello?"

She paused briefly, without speaking a word.

The man again said, "Hello?" a second time.

Still, she didn't respond.

She realized the man on the other end would soon hang up if she didn't take her chance. She regained her courage and replied, "Yes! Hello. Um, my name is Barbara Harding, and I was wondering if you would help me find my missing daughter." Her direct approach surprised even her, and she waited for a response.

After what seemed like a lifetime, the man calmly asked, "What did you say your name was?"

"Barbara Harding," she responded.

The stranger seemed annoyed by her call and said, "Lady, how did you get this phone number?"

She didn't reply at first. Then she said, "I overheard you talking with Jack Danbury, the detective. When he dialed your phone number, it appeared on the phone's dial pad. I looked down and memorized it. I was desperate to talk to you. Please, I want to ask for your help in finding my daughter. I'm sorry, but I don't know what else to do. The police don't seem to be able to help me. You're my last hope."

Somewhere from the recesses of her soul, Barbara added, "You see, I slew the evil. Now it needs to release my daughter."

Where had those words come from? she wondered to herself even as she waited for Sterling's response.

There was silence on the other end, but she knew he was still on the line. She waited for any response at all—for something to happen.

"Come tomorrow morning at this address: 410 East Forty-Third Street in New York City. Come at precisely eight o'clock, and ask for Sterling."

Then, without warning, the phone went dead.

Barbara stood with the receiver in her hand until the high-pitched sound became too annoying, then hung up. Quickly jotting down the address, she placed it neatly away in her purse and stood in shock and apprehension.

Suddenly feeling exhilarated, she walked over to the kitchen sink and started washing the dishes. Within her spirit came the understanding she would meet this man and beg for his help. But he was a stranger—how would she know she could trust him? Was he even a genuine psychic or a phony? She had more questions than answers.

Meeting someone downtown was something she had never done before, something out of the ordinary. What she had just agreed to do made her somewhat frightened. Driving to the city was reckless; she needed to contemplate this journey more carefully. *Maybe I shouldn't show up and should abandon the whole idea*, she thought.

Having errands to complete before Mark got home, Barbara ran to the grocery store and dry cleaner; the rest of the afternoon was spent on chores around the house. Before she knew it, Mark arrived home.

"What's for dinner?" he asked.

Dinner! She hadn't given it any thought. She smiled and replied, "Whatever your heart desires, my love, but dinner has to wait. I have to run over to Susan's to pick up Rachel."

"There's no need," Mark replied while holding Rachel's heavy backpack in his hand. "I already picked Rachel up on my way home. When we pulled into the driveway, she saw Debbie playing outside and wanted to talk to her. I reminded her that she had homework to do, but she promised not to play very long. Here's her backpack. Where should I put it?"

"Just put it on the kitchen table. She likes to do her homework there while I'm cooking dinner. By the way, do you still have that street map of New York City?"

"Yes, it's around here somewhere. In the den, I think. Why do you want a map of the city? You know we don't travel there unless we have a good reason. It's not safe downtown."

"I'm interested in knowing the location of a certain street, that's all."

"What street are you talking about?" Mark asked.

"Oh, I don't know; it was something like Forty-Third Street in New York City."

"Hmm, okay." A moment later Mark suggested. "I'll tell you what. You figure out dinner, and I'll see if I can find that street for you."

"That sounds good to me," she responded, opening the refrigerator. She took out a pound of hamburger and began to prepare dinner.

Mark set Rachel's backpack on the table and went into the den to search for the map. He couldn't understand her reasons for wanting the address. It was just something she wanted to know—that's all that mattered.

When he walked into the den, he turned on the light and

looked around. An oak roll-top desk was against the wall overflowing with paperwork, including the monthly mortgage and utility bills stuffed inside the wooden slots. Mark thought the map was in one of the drawers, but which one? He began pulling open drawers and rummaged through a stack of magazines, including *Home Interiors* and *Hunting and Rifles* but found no map.

When he reached the large bottom drawers, he found electrical plugs and wiring switches, large mailing envelopes with bubble-pack linings, computer paper, and ink cartridges but no map.

Dammit, he thought, *where is that map book?* Mark tried to remember when he'd used it last. Suddenly, it occurred to him: The last time he traveled downtown was to an appliance warehouse to pick up a new dishwasher pump. "I bet it's still in my pickup," he said aloud, shut the drawer, and walked outside.

Mark opened the passenger door to his truck, then his glove box. There, lying inside, was the city map book. He walked back to the house and into the kitchen where the aroma of cooking hamburgers filled his nostrils. He turned to his wife and said, "Whatever we're having, it sure does smell good."

Seeing the map book in his hands, Barbara smiled in response and said, "Dinner will be ready in about twenty minutes. Can you show me where Forty-Third Street is?"

"Sure, give me a minute to look up the address," he replied.

Sitting down at the kitchen table, with Barbara looking over his shoulder, he went to the index at the back of the book and found Forty-Third Street on page 26, section B11.

Then he turned to the page and pointed at the street, which ran in an easterly direction through some of the inner city's forgotten thoroughfares.

Mark sat back in his chair, ran his hands through his hair,

and proclaimed, "Well, I'm not sure I would dare to venture down there. It's a place where the police don't dare visit. I remember reading about that area. Someone did a story a year ago about the abandoned neighborhoods throughout the city. They have their secret societies, all governed by kingpins who have complete control over what goes on inside their territory. Cross one of those honchos, and they'll never find your body again!"

Barbara looked a little sheepish and smiled nervously while saying, "Well, dinner should be ready soon. Why don't you go wash up? I'll get Rachel at her friend's house."

"Great idea," Mark answered. "I'm hungry for whatever it is you're cooking. It sure does smell good!" He got up from the table, planted a kiss on Barbara's cheek, and left the room.

With Mark gone, she had a little time to study the map more closely and determine the best route to get to Forty-Third Street. She had been downtown on her own but never in that part of the city before. It was some distance from the interstate, and she would have to travel through many winding streets to get there, which concerned her greatly.

Just then Rachel came prancing into the house and said, "Hey, Mom. What's cooking?"

"Just some Sloppy Joe's. It's almost ready. Why don't you set the table?" Barbara suggested.

"Sure, Mom," Rachel replied.

She walked over to the cupboard, took out the plates, and began to set the table. Without realizing it she laid a plate for Melissa and stared at it thoughtfully. Leaving it, she continued to set the table and turned to her mother.

"All done."

"Thank you, honey," Barbara said. Browning the hamburger and adding tomato sauce to the pan, she thought, *What have I gotten myself into now?*

Chapter 12

Barbara could hardly sleep that night for fear of the unknown that lay ahead. Going downtown on her own made her nervous. She made arrangements that night with Susan to keep Rachel after school, thinking she might get back home late.

Before she and Mark went to bed, she informed him that she had an errand early the following day, and he would have to get Rachel on the school bus for her. Before she left the house, she made herself some toast and coffee. Taking the coffee in a to-go mug, she gathered her belongings and headed out to the garage to start her car. Inside she found a note taped to the steering wheel from Mark that read: "Please look in the glove box. It's there for your protection. Be careful. Please. Love you."

Curious, Barbara opened the glove box. Inside, resting on the car's registration and insurance envelope, was Mark's .38 revolver. Seeing the weapon made her feel safer, even though she'd only shot it twice at her husband's insistence.

Nervously, she inserted the key in the ignition and started the car. The reality of what she was doing hit home. She wished there was another way, but it was too late to back out now. The thought of Melissa being tortured drove her on. She headed to the interstate and drove south.

Nearly an hour later the tall structures of New York City came into view. Fighting traffic the whole way, she soon saw her turnoff among the multitude of busy freeway off-ramps. Exiting, she came to a signal, stopped, and waited for the light to change. As she waited a homeless person stood on the street corner, begging for change. His cardboard cutout displayed the words: "Help a brother out. God bless you!"

When the light turned green, Barbara rolled her eyes at the man as he waved back at her, knowing she must not have approved of him. She made her way downtown to the sleazy and forgotten part of the city. The scenery changed, and the buildings and houses became uglier the further into the metropolis she drove.

At Forty-Third Street she made a right-hand turn and followed the addresses down the street, carefully observing the numbers on the buildings until she saw the faded number 410 on a brick building. A broken-down car with flat tires was abandoned in front of the building, making it difficult to park. Driving a short distance down the street, she parked her car, got out, and walked down the sidewalk. The sun's brilliance hardly penetrated the roads below, causing shadows of different angles between the buildings. Walking toward its entrance, she glanced down again at the little scrap of paper to verify the address.

She stopped for a moment and stared cautiously at the old building, trying to decide whether or not it was safe to enter. Looking around the empty street, she became increasingly frightened and hesitant to walk inside. Glancing down at her watch, she saw that it was 7:55 a.m.—five minutes early. Should she wait inside her car? Everything around her seemed cold and creepy; she wasn't sure what to do.

She noticed someone approaching. She studied the stranger: an elderly lady, all alone, pulling a little cart behind her. As the woman got closer, Barbara guessed her to be in her early seventies. She seemed in a hurry as if she was running late for an appointment. As she walked by, Barbara overheard her say, "I'm late. I should have had the office open already."

The woman struggled up the stairs of Number 410, still pulling the little cart. When she reached the landing, she took out a key from her coat pocket, unlocked the door, and briskly walked inside.

Cautiously, Barbara followed behind and watched as she continued down a hallway that led to a small office. Barbara's first impression was that no one had used this vacant space for some time, based on the dirty windows and the dusty floor that left the woman's footprints wherever she walked.

The old lady disappeared from view. The only evidence left behind was her footprints and cart tracks on the dusty floor. Barbara stood alone in the dark, musty hallway. She noticed the other offices located on the first floor showed no sign of occupancy. Each one had a dark wooden door with a unique number painted in gold, from one to five.

As she stood there observing the rooms and wondering what business they provided, she heard a distant door slam shut from behind a wood-paneled wall. It sounded to her as if someone were opening another door somewhere else.

Looking down at her watch, she saw it was ten minutes after eight. The moment had arrived when she must decide whether to stay or leave. Feeling like an animal trapped in a maze, she wasn't sure what to do. Should she try one of the doors to see if it opened or wait for the woman to reappear? As Barbara pondered her next move, she heard a door unlock behind office number three.

She took a deep breath and walked inside as the door opened with a loud creaking noise that announced her presence to whoever was there. Sitting behind a wire panel was the woman.

"Yes, may I help you?" the woman asked.

Barbara assertively walked up to the counter and replied, "I would like to see Sterling, if I may."

The lady didn't respond at first. She just wrote something down on what looked like an appointment log and then politely asked, "Whom may I say is waiting?"

"Barbara Harding is my name. I have an appointment with a man who calls himself Sterling,"

"Okay, I'll let him know. Have a seat in the lobby, please."

The room held only three pieces of furniture: two rickety wooden chairs and an old sofa against the wall. Hanging on the opposite wall was an antique clock made of decorative brass. The numbers were big, and the hour and minute hands were thin, beautiful brass strips that came to a point, like the tip of an arrow. Its body was round except for the long, brass pendulum that swung from side to side.

In the room were two small frosted-glass windows that allowed only the slightest amount of light to penetrate the waiting area. Overhead two dirty lamps mounted in the ceiling provided some needed light in the small space.

Without saying anything else Barbara removed her jacket and sat down, preparing herself to be called any moment. She glanced up at the old clock; it was twenty minutes past eight. Already she felt anxious to leave and go home. Still, she sat and watched for any movement from within the small office that would announce Sterling had arrived. But, to her disappointment, the long minutes turned to an hour as the morning ticked slowly away.

Barbara had nothing but time on her hands, and she sat patiently. The first hour passed; still, she waited. The old lady behind the cage hadn't called out her name or made any attempt to talk to her. Barbara remained persistent and sat quietly in the dusty old room until the clock chimed 10 a.m.

Her patience had run thin, and she got up from her seat and approached the cage where the older woman sat.

"Does Sterling even know that I am waiting to see him?" Barbara politely asked.

The old lady nodded and smiled. "Sterling will see you shortly. Please be patient just a little longer."

Barbara reluctantly agreed, pointing out the fact she'd waited for two hours already. Feeling desperate, Barbara began to question the old lady. She asked her if this Sterling character was going to help find her missing daughter.

The old woman looked back at her with a sympathetic expression and replied, "I don't know, dearie. Now please have a seat. I'm sure Sterling will be calling you soon."

Barbara felt somewhat foolish for asking if Sterling would help her. Regardless, she'd had nothing to lose by asking the question, if only to see the woman's reaction. Quietly returning to the sofa, Barbara waited while the old clock sounded the passing hours that now seemed to drag along. Occasionally, she would hear an outburst of shouting from outside the building or a single car racing down the street. But besides that, the only sound she heard came from the clock.

Chapter 13

When the clock announced 11 a.m., the timepiece played a melodious song as the hammer struck tiny bells. In response the older woman, who had been crocheting a blanket, got up from her seat, walked over, and took a bagged lunch from her cart. She returned to her chair, opened a wrapper, and started eating a homemade sandwich.

By that time Barbara was feeling hungry. The sandwich the woman was eating looked delicious. She hadn't brought anything with her to have for lunch because she hadn't expected to wait so long. Unfortunately, she would remain hungry. The thought of getting into her car to search for someplace to eat didn't appeal to her. Instead, she rummaged through her purse for something edible, found a roll of Life Savers, and quietly sucked on them as the afternoon ticked away. An uncomfortable feeling began to creep in. She had to find a bathroom. The morning coffee was affecting her. She rose to her feet, walked over to the old lady at the counter, and interrupted her.

"Excuse me, but do you have a bathroom nearby I can use?"

"Yes, we have a bathroom in the back of the office. Just come through the door next to me, and you can't miss it."

"Thank you," Barbara responded and made her way to

the back office.

Seeing a door marked "Ladies' Room," she entered. Inside she was surprised to see the bathroom was clean and neat. Above the toilet sat a cute little plant on a wooden shelf that gave a homey feeling to the room.

When she finished, she walked out of the bathroom and examined the office area more carefully. There was only one other door, partly illuminated by a weak light coming through its frosted glass window.

Barbara guessed the office must belong to Sterling and stood there for a moment listening for any movement from within. After hearing no sound inside the office, she thought, *This Sterling character hasn't even been here. This whole thing is nothing but a waste of my time.*

As she contemplated the door, the old woman asked, "Do you feel any better?"

Barbara turned and saw the old lady had been watching her the entire time.

"Yes, thank you," Barbara replied.

The woman was still sitting in her chair, finishing the last of her sandwich.

Wanting some answers, Barbara said, "Excuse me, but is Sterling even in his office?"

"No, not yet."

Disgusted, Barbara asked, "Will you please tell me why you haven't said that Sterling isn't here?"

The old lady smiled and replied, "Sterling will be along shortly. I'm sure of it. Now go ahead and have a seat back in the lobby, dearie."

Barbara replied, trying her best to remain calm, "I've been waiting here for over four hours already."

"Yes, I know, but sometimes you have to wait patiently for things that are worth having. This old world may be fast-paced, but there are times when you have to stop and smell the roses, watch the birds making their nests, and not be in such a hurry for quick results," she proclaimed as if offering pearls of wisdom.

Barbara reluctantly returned to the lobby and again took a seat on the sofa. Feeling upset and miserable, she contemplated if using this so-called psychic to find Melissa was a good idea after all. Her anger grew as she fought off both hunger and her emotions as the clock slowly ticked away the afternoon.

Shortly after the clock announced one p.m., the office's front door opened, and in walked an older man in tattered clothing. Slowly, he strolled over to the old lady and asked to speak to Sterling.

The woman politely asked him to have a seat in the lobby.

"What's your name, sir? I'll let Sterling know you're here."

"Mr. Gillet," he answered in a shaky voice.

The stranger got comfortable in the chair, then glanced at Barbara and smiled. She smiled back, studying him more closely but not speaking. She didn't want to encourage conversation.

He looked like a street person. His torn clothing was old and filthy. He had a long, gray beard, and she could smell his body odor from across the room. As she watched he wiped his nose on his dirty coat sleeve, making her want to gag. She was confident he was of no interest to her and was glad he'd chosen to sit alone on the chair, not share the sofa with her. He was far enough away that she could ignore his presence and remain focused on watching the clock ticking away the afternoon.

Another hour passed; the clock sounded the familiar melody, announcing that it was now two o'clock. Barbara was growing ravenous, and her patience was running thin.

Presently, the stranger across from her began to snore. Between the man's snoring and the constant waiting, she didn't know whether to cry or scream, but she was determined to wait it out.

She studied the stranger more carefully. As he slumped in the chair, snoring away as if at home, he appeared calm and as innocent as a child, as if he didn't have a care in the world. She found herself becoming a bit curious about this man's reason for coming to see a psychic.

What if all this is just a waste of time and there's no Sterling after all? I should get up and leave; seeing a psychic for help is a silly idea. However, still determined to see this finished, she again focused her attention on the sleeping man. Was something sinister going on? Maybe this homeless man's visit somehow involved money. Her imagination went into overdrive. Perhaps he was blackmailing Sterling. Perhaps the homeless man had some information that would send Sterling to jail for the rest of his life. What if this man had seen Sterling kill someone? Or maybe Sterling was a robber, and this old guy was his accomplice.

Barbara stared at his face to see if he looked like he could be a bank robber, paying close attention to his eyes. She tried to remember what they'd looked like before he'd closed them and had begun his annoying snoring.

She became frustrated because she couldn't remember what color they were. Were they brown or blue or hazel? She began to fume. Psychic or no psychic, if this older man starts any trouble, I'm racing for the door and getting out of here as fast as I can.

Barbara remembered a small container of pepper spray mounted on her keychain. Having it made her feel somewhat safer. She would keep her guard up, not allow herself to relax around this old guy. *Who knows? He may be harmless, but I will put up a fight if I need to defend myself.* She looked over at the old lady who was also inert—the woman couldn't help her if the old geezer tried something funny. Barbara was alone.

The next hour passed quickly and in some way felt different. Maybe it was the distraction of watching the sleeping man for any sign of trouble, or perhaps she was becoming used to waiting around the old office—though she couldn't say that was the case for her sore rear end. The clock ticked away another hour and then another. Finally, the realization set in that Sterling wasn't going to show up. If he were, he would have been there by now.

As she wondered how much more time she was going to waste, the old lady closed her little window and locked it into place. A moment later she appeared in the lobby with her cart, turned around, and locked the door behind her. Turning back around, she faced Barbara and said, "Well, dearie, it looks like Sterling won't be able to see you today after all."

Unable to contain her frustration and anger, Barbara shot to her feet. "Well, when you see this man Sterling," she shrieked, "you can tell him for me that I'll be back here tomorrow and the next day and even the next day after that, as long as it takes before he will agree to help me, damn him!"

Roused by her tirade, the older man awoke from his slumber as Barbara, overcome by emotion, broke out in tears and said, "I don't give a damn what this Sterling guy is doing that is so important he couldn't see me. I need his help finding my daughter Melissa."

Shattered, she fell to the floor, weeping, a broken woman at the end of her rope.

The old lady stood there in shock, unmoving as Barbara remained on the floor, sobbing.

Suddenly, a man's voice spoke up and said, "That's all I

wanted to hear; your own words proclaiming to the world you would do anything to get your daughter back."

Barbara stopped crying. Raising her head, she looked in the direction of the sleeping man. He wasn't sleeping now but stared back at her, his eyes filled with compassion. He stood, walked over, reached out his hand, and helped her to her feet.

Barbara looked intently into his eyes and asked, "What did you just say?"

"Barbara, I'm Sterling."

Chapter 14

"You're Sterling?" Shock showed on her face.

"Yes, I am," he replied in a soft voice. "I must ask you to please forgive me for what I have put you through. You must understand I had no other way to find out how far you were willing to go to find your daughter."

"My daughter?" she responded. "What do you know about Melissa?"

"I only know what the police have discovered in their investigation. Nothing more at this time, but…." He paused and chose his following words carefully. "I know she's still alive."

Shocked, Barbara wondered why he would say something that bold. She believed in her heart Melissa was still alive, but why did he? "You think Melissa is still alive?"

"Yes, I do. I cannot explain it to you in a way that you would understand," he answered while proceeding to remove the smelly clothing from his body.

Once he had taken off the dirty old coat and pants, Barbara saw he was dressed in dark slacks, a white shirt, and dark socks. The old lady watched him disrobe with little surprise, and when Sterling asked for his shoes, she happily reached into her cart and handed them over.

After slipping them on his feet, he began to laugh.

"Well, I don't need this old beard anymore, do I?" he said, then peeled it off his face, exposing a clean-shaven jaw beneath. Before her, much to Barbara's surprise, stood a handsome man who looked to be in his early thirties. He had jet-black hair and the bluest eyes, which reminded her of dark crystal pools, and a smile that seemed warm and inviting. She was completely taken aback by his appearance.

Funny, she thought, *I once believed him to be a frail old geezer, but now he is young and good-looking.*

"You see, Barbara, I have seen—or, rather, felt—Melissa's aura. It still burns brightly in this world. That's why I'm telling you she is still alive. Unfortunately, I must also inform you that I cannot help you any further in your search," Sterling answered with regret.

"What do you mean?" Barbara asked, disappointed.

Sterling's stare went right through her; she felt helpless to argue, surrendering to his will as he held her attention with his gaze.

"You see, I'm already helping another mother such as yourself. She, too, has lost a child. Just as you have lost your daughter, she has lost her son. I've been staying with her family as my way to capture the missing child's sense of awareness at a place familiar to him where he had found comfort."

Sterling explained that when he agreed to help someone find a missing loved one, he stayed in the living space where the individual felt safest. "You see, in that place I'll be able to connect with the missing child. I can feel the child's life force that remains behind, even though that person has gone missing—in much the same way a dog can smell the scent of someone's trace left behind."

He also explained that staying with the family filled in the blanks of someone's life, and it was there where he could connect with the lost soul. "Two completely separate beings somehow connected in that place of love and comfort. That's how I can learn what happened to that person."

Forgetting about her hunger and sore body, Barbara felt a new, more substantial confidence than anything she had felt previously. She knew that together she and Sterling would find Melissa. All the needless worry had vanished with his announcement that her daughter was still alive. She was ready to surrender and put her trust in this tall, dark stranger, accepting the fact that for now she could do nothing else except wait for him to solve the other case.

Sterling offered to walk her out to her car. She followed him out of the old office and into the street, trailed closely by the mature woman who had packed all of Sterling's dirty clothing in her cart and was taking it with her—no doubt to be used at another time to test the courage of some other unsuspecting parent.

"What about your assistant?" Barbara asked.

Looking at the woman, Sterling said, "She'll be okay. You needn't worry about her."

At the bottom of the stairs they paused on the sidewalk briefly and looked back at the older adult as she struggled down the steps, her tired old body managing each one with some effort. Once the old lady was standing on the sidewalk, she approached Sterling. He stood patiently waiting, knowing that if he offered any help, she would be offended.

"Will you need me tomorrow?"

Staring down at her tenderly, Sterling responded, "No, thank you. That'll be enough for now. If I need you, I'll call. A check will appear in your mailbox tomorrow."

Sterling bid her a good evening and closely observed her trail off, pulling her cart behind. Barbara didn't know where she was going and felt terrible seeing her all alone in such a harsh environment.

Just then something caught her eye. Looking more

closely, she saw the lady was no longer unaccompanied; Barbara could faintly see a figure in the shadows that appeared to be following her.

Sterling, seeing Barbara's reaction, announced, "You don't know this world for what it truly is; only what it appears to be. Things here are not what they seem. Martha, whose husband was the fire chief many years ago, refused to leave her home, even though all her friends abandoned her when her husband died. She remains, having no one else to care for her."

Barbara didn't understand and asked, "What do you mean?"

"You see the old, broken-down buildings and people the way everyone else does: as broken-down societies in which everyone inside the old dwellings is in constant danger, bad people are out to inflict pain and possibly death upon the unsuspecting innocent. What you fail to see is the natural order of things here in this neighborhood. The ones who control the streets have in place certain safeguards. One such owner is a friend of mine who owes me much. Barbara, it's time to go. Will you please follow me?"

Regardless of the destination, Barbara began to trust this stranger and followed him without hesitation. On the way she looked up and asked, "Who was the shadowy figure?"

"She is never alone here and is in no danger. As I said before, her protector owes a debt of gratitude that can't ever be repaid. She is at peace here among the ruins of a bygone era—that is, of course, unless someone dares to upset the apple cart. I wouldn't wish that tragedy on my worst enemies."

They approached Barbara's car, still parked on the lonely street. It showed no sign of damage of any kind and was in the same condition as when she'd left it. Sterling stuck out his hand and shook Barbara's.

"Goodbye until we meet again. I will contact you as soon as I can."

"How soon?" she asked desperately.

"I'm not sure. But time is what's most important here. I hate to waste my time on unfruitful pursuits that go nowhere; you should know that, Barbara," Sterling answered.

"Where do we begin?" she asked. "If my daughter is still alive, then surely there must not be much time left!"

"Barbara, I have a choice in this matter: to abandon my current mission to help you find your daughter. But you should know as you ask this of me that a mother, much like yourself, sits alone at night, crying for her child. It's my cross to bear, and I desperately search out the missing clues for loved ones to be reunited. But there are those rare occasions when I'm unable to help for obvious reasons, you understand?"

"Yes, the person you've been searching for has died. Still, I believe you can help me; I have no one else," Barbara proclaimed.

Sterling, looking pleased, announced, "Look down the street and observe."

As Barbara turned to look, she caught a glimmer of light appearing out of a window, far away in one of the old buildings. While studying the lit apartment, Sterling secretly dropped something small inside Barbara's coat pocket.

Looking at her, he declared, "You see, I told you she would be safe."

Barbara remarked, "Yes, you're right. I see that now." She walked back to her car, got inside, and started the engine. Then she rolled down the passenger window as if to say something else.

Sterling approached and said, "I have one favor to ask you. Do not change your daughter's bedroom in any way. Leave her bedroom exactly as it was the day she disappeared.

Can you do that for me?"

"Yes, of course. I haven't changed anything in Melissa's room since the day she went missing. I don't plan on changing it either; when she comes back home, I want her to see it's just like she left it."

"Fine. I'll be notifying you when I'm ready to begin your daughter's search. I honestly feel it won't be long until we meet again." He looked away, then added, "There's something sinister I feel about the way the child disappeared, and I fear for the little boy's safety, too. I shouldn't say anything more than that."

Before he walked away, he looked back at her with serious intent. "Let nothing in this world rob you of the belief that your daughter is still alive, no matter where the attacks originate. I have provided assistance to help you in times of weakness."

Stepping back from the car, he stood on the sidewalk, silent and unmoving, as she drove out of the city toward home.

Feeling surreal, she began to think none of what she had just experienced had happened at all, as if meeting Sterling, the mysterious stranger, was something that had happened to characters in a book or movie.

When she arrived at the Bernsteins' house, it was close to six o'clock in the evening. After parking in their driveway, she shut off the car engine and sat there for a moment before getting out, thinking of what to say if Susan asked about where she had gone. Barbara decided they would have to discuss the matter later, perhaps over lunch. For now she would give her a condensed version. Thinking about Melissa, Barbara began to cry. After some time of releasing the pent-up emotion, she looked in the car mirror. She wiped away the mascara that had run, deciding the red in her eyes could be blamed on air pollution if anyone asked.

She got out of her car and walked up the steps to the front

door. As she was about to knock, she was startled by the sound of Susan's voice calling her. Turning around, she saw Susan coming from the backyard, tugging a large trash bin through the side gate.

"So, how did your appointment downtown go?" Susan asked.

"Everything went fine, I guess. It was better than I expected," Barbara replied. "Susan, if it's all the same to you, let's meet for lunch later this week to discuss it further. I'm beat and don't want to get into it right now."

"Meet for lunch? That's a splendid idea. Just let me know when and where," Susan replied excitedly.

As they entered the house together, their conversation became more relaxed. Feeling exhausted, Barbara said nothing further about her trip to the big city or her daughter's disappearance. Instead, they discussed Susan's rose garden and what she planned on planting that spring.

After a few minutes Barbara asked, "Is Rachel about ready?"

"Yes, I believe so. Rachel's completing the last of her homework and should be just about done."

Barbara called out to Rachel and told her to get her things together. Turning to Susan, she thanked her again for picking up her daughter after school and began telling her goodbye. She was anxious to leave; it had been a long day, and she just wanted to get home to relax as soon as possible.

While she waited for Rachel, Barbara reached into her coat pocket for her car keys. She felt something strange beside her keys: a small, smooth, round object. Barbara lifted it out of her pocket and stared at it, trying to decide what it might be. Surprised by its weight, she held it aloft inside the dimly lit foyer. When she switched on the hallway light to examine it more closely, the light reflected onto the object's many facets, sending off beams of light of different tints of brightness into every darkened space within the entryway.

"What do you have there?" said Susan.

"I'm not sure what it is myself—or where it came from," Barbara replied.

Both women stood mesmerized by its radiance as they tried to imagine what was causing the light to shine as it did. They finally concluded the object must have internal batteries and could be one of Rachel's toys or some small trinket she had borrowed from one of her classmates.

Barbara dropped it back into her coat to discuss the matter with Rachel when they got home.

Again, she called for Rachel to get moving. Susan called out to her as well, as the pair stood waiting in the foyer. Finally, Rachel appeared, dragging her backpack behind her, and followed her mother out to the car. As usual Rachel crawled into the backseat. Barbara thanked Susan again and, with a final hug, told her that she would give her a call tomorrow.

At home Mark's truck was already in the driveway, blocking her access to the garage. As she and Rachel headed toward the house, she noticed the garage door was partially open; Mark was inside, working on their broken lawnmower. It was half disassembled, with parts scattered about his workbench. Country-and-western music played so loudly he hadn't heard them pull up.

Barbara approached him with disappointment in her voice and asked, "Are you working on that old mower again?"

Mark turned around to see his frustrated wife and replied, "Yes, I am. I want to have it ready for spring."

Too tired to argue, Barbara decided to buy a new lawnmower soon and walked into the house with Rachel following her. Inside Rachel tossed her coat onto the floor and dashed toward her bedroom to watch her favorite cartoons. Catching her before she had gotten too far, Barbara said, "You know that doesn't belong there. Go hang it up in the closet, please."

Rachel turned around and grudgingly did as she was told, then ran down the hallway to her room and disappeared.

Barbara hung up her coat as well, then headed to her bedroom to get comfortable before dinner. A thought occurred to her: *Perhaps I should take a closer look at that mysterious crystal I found in my coat.* Returning to the closet, she reached into her coat pocket, feeling her fingers rub against the small object. Its surface felt warm at the touch, which seemed odd.

She lifted it out and stared at it. Amazingly, it was burning even more brightly than when she'd been at Susan's house.

It captivated her imagination. She felt curious about the object and wondered about its origin. *I must ask Rachel immediately,* she thought. Besides, she wanted to ask her why she'd placed it in her pocket. Then another thought occurred to her: *What if Rachel wasn't the one who put it in my coat? Who did?*

She hurried down the hallway with the crystal in her hand. As she passed Melissa's bedroom, the crystal began to glow brighter and brighter. Pausing just outside the door, she stopped and didn't move. The crystal burned with such intensity that she could hardly look at it.

She held her palm flat, the object resting in the center. She was compelled to walk into Melissa's bedroom. As she took a step inside, the crystal's light became blindingly bright, reaching into the darkest corners of the room, filling every murky space with beams of shimmering light. She realized with a shock that she hadn't turned on any lights; the object glowed more brightly with each step she took.

As she stood silently watching the effects of the light against the blackest of the shadows, something moved! Frightened, she wanted to run away but instead stood transfixed as a pair of long, bony arms reached out from under Melissa's bed.

She somehow knew the dark, shadowy figure was trying to crawl from some other place into this world. As she watched in silent horror, it slowly pulled its body upward from under the bed. A dark and menacing fog swirled and grew until it assumed the shape of a tiny human skull with two bulging eyes embedded in deep sockets, eagerly watching Barbara with keen interest.

Frozen in fear and unable to move or retreat, she stood perfectly still. The dark body changed, blending within the blackness in front of her—this thing was death itself.

Slowly, it rose from the floor and became erect—alive. The air in Melissa's bedroom was becoming frigid, and Barbara shivered in the sudden cold. All she could do was to stand immobile and watch intently as the apparition came to life.

The body of the ghastly image was almost transparent, with dark, oily skin. Now that it was upright, Barbara could see it stood close to six feet tall with a body as black as a moonless night.

The creature unfolded two broad, enormous wings; they stretched halfway across the room. To her horror, it opened its mouth wide and let out an ear-piercing scream as if it had just been wounded. Flinching, she clamped her hands over her ears.

Questions flooded her mind. Why is this creature here in Melissa's bedroom? What can this all possibly mean? Only one thing mattered: How could she defeat this creature that was threatening her life?

The answer to that question, she realized, was in the palm of her hand. As the dark demon fully materialized, the small object she held burned ever more brightly. As the entity grew in strength and magnification, the burning brightness in the room increased as well. She somehow understood this object was inflicting the pain the creature felt. What kind of weapon was it? More importantly, if this small object caused this beast such enormous pain, how could she use it to defeat the monster?

The light restrained the creature, but it fought against it. In one final attempt to get at her, the creature stuck out its long, skeletal fingers; its razor-sharp nails tried to stop the incandescent light from penetrating its hazy body. Still, every time it drew closer to harm her, the shining brilliance from the crystal object became even brighter and held the creature back.

Inside herself something suddenly changed; she wouldn't surrender to her fears. She would show this creature no mercy or weakness. She stepped toward the being, holding the light before her. As she did, the creature's menacing shape began to change. It was no longer the threatening being it once had been, and it began to draw inward. Its once proudly displayed wings collapsed into its body. Its form seemed to lower in submission; the strange creature looked as though it bowed before her.

The incandescent light from the small crystal penetrated deep into its dark body as it began to creep backward under Melissa's bed, retreating into the world in which it lived. As it withdrew, it took on a much smaller form than before.

Her courage renewed, Barbara took another step closer. As she looked upon the inky body, it shrank to nothingness and disappeared from her sight.

She took a deep breath. It was gone. But she knew it had only been subdued for now. It had had no choice but to retreat to the abyss of its home, in that other world where darkness lived.

But would it be back?

Barbara was both shaken and astonished. What had just taken place inside Melissa's room was a complete mystery.

Why in the world was that creature inside Melissa's bedroom? What type of creature was it anyway? What brought it here? And what is this crystal thing all about? *I don't understand!*

Standing there alone, staring at the thing in her hand, she wondered how this small intricate object could derive such authority over evil. The object's light diminished with the black devil gone until it remained a soft, tiny, shining orb. Expecting the worst, Barbara decided perhaps the crystal should sit on her daughter's dresser for the time being if that creature decided to come back for a visit.

Suddenly, she remembered Rachel. She was alone in her bedroom. Frantically, she ran to Rachel's bedroom and burst inside. Rachel sat on her bed watching her favorite cartoons with the volume turned up so loudly that she was incapable of hearing the phantom's scream from the next room.

Instead of doing her homework, she was captivated by her favorite television program. Busted, Rachel reached for the remote, shut off the set, picked up her nearby math book, and began to study her math problems. Looking at her with relief, Barbara broke out in laughter and plopped down on the corner of her bed, collapsing from the fear of losing her other daughter.

Thinking her mother weird, Rachel just looked up at her, trying to see the humor in what she had done.

"It's all right. You're not in trouble. Come here, baby."

Rachel quickly joined her mother on her bed. Barbara gripped her tightly, happy to know Rachel was safe. She somehow, knew Rachel, too, could've been taken away by that mysterious creature. As they sat together on the bed, Barbara held onto her daughter until she heard Mark enter the house.

After hanging his jacket on the back of one of the dining room chairs, Mark walked into the kitchen and was about to wash the dirt and grime from his hands when he heard his wife and daughter come into the room.

"What's for dinner?" he asked with a smile.

He was overwhelmed with kisses and tight embraces before he got any response. Chuckling, he returned the affection, hugging his daughter warmly and kissing his wife. Then, looking directly into Barbara's eyes, he repeated his question: "What's for dinner?"

"Whatever you want," Barbara replied.

Feeling cheerful, he announced, "I have a better idea. Why not go out and grab a bite to eat instead of making something at home?"

"Yes, let's go. I don't feel like making dinner anyway," Barbara approved.

Turning to Rachel, she said, "Go, get your coat. We're leaving."

She wanted nothing more than to get away as quickly as possible. Grabbing her coat and purse, she ushered her family out the door. Once outside Barbara examined the interior of their home for anything suspicious. All was tranquil, and she saw nothing out of the ordinary except for the pale light of the tiny crystal glowing in the window of her daughter's bedroom. The soft light penetrated the darkness within the entire house.

The light was protection against evil, but how had it gotten into her pocket? After running to lock the front door, she raced out to get into her car. As Mark drove the car, Barbara turned around to look at the house for a second time. Somehow the creature had been defeated by the crystal. That was encouraging, but what about the next time she encountered the spirit? Will she have the courage and cunning to win that battle?

Each question only brought more problems. Barbara tried to listen to Mark's comments about his job, nodding in agreement as he explained the upcoming changes at his aerospace plant. Upper management wanted everyone to take a pay cut. At other times she would've listened and sympathized; but now she was fixated on that hideous creature, wondering what she would have done if it had gotten hold of Rachel.

The crystal must have come from Sterling, not Rachel. It wasn't a toy; she knew that much. Sterling had known she would need it for protection, but why hadn't he told her what to expect? *Why didn't he warn me that something like that devil was lurking in Melissa's room?* She remembered his words. "There was just no other way to find out how far you were willing to go to find your daughter." Does this mean I have to fight demons and ghosts and who knows what else to get Melissa back?

Looking behind her once more at the dimly lit streets of her neighborhood, she caught the last glimpse of their house among the others in the sparsely lit community. Anger and determination filled her as she made a vow to herself: "I will fight whoever or whatever I have to so I can get Melissa back, even if it means I have to sacrifice my life to do it."

Clueless about the dangers his wife was facing, Mark drove to the restaurant, complaining about his job and oblivious to what she had seen in their once happy home.

Chapter 15

After returning home from dropping Rachel off at school, Barbara called Susan to discuss plans for lunch. Susan happily suggested they meet downtown at one of her favorite cafés. Arriving a few minutes early, Barbara reviewed the lunch menu, but the events of the previous evening haunted her mind.

She had somehow exorcised a demonic monster and sent it back into the black shadows from whence it came. Since that day all seemed normal and calm; could it really be so easy? If the creature returned, she would at least have the crystal to battle it; she'd left it on her daughter's nightstand to block any attempts by the ominous shadow to regain entry into the house.

Dismissing devils and monsters from her mind, Barbara thought of Susan instead. Susan was trustworthy if nothing else. She could count on her for anything. Over the years Susan proved herself to be the strength Barbara needed when she felt weak.

One particular incident came to mind. Some years ago Mark had been in an automobile accident; Barbara received a call from the police and hurriedly left her office. When she arrived at the hospital, she called Susan.

Without hesitation Susan took their daughters to her house to care for them while Barbara attended to Mark's needs. A few days later Susan brought the girls to the hospital to see their father. Afterward, she continued to help with them while Mark was recovering. Mark's parents lived out of state so Susan and John had taken over the role of grandparents. There was no one Barbara would rather trust in an emergency.

Looking up, she saw Susan standing at the door of the café and waved to draw her attention to her corner booth. After the two friends hugged, Susan began to complain about the difficulty of parking downtown, saying she wished they would build more public parking.

"I know what you mean," Barbara protested, "but for now enough of that. Let's order lunch."

Looking around the café, she spotted a young waitress chewing bubble gum and waved her over. The young woman introduced herself as Martha.

"I'll be your server today—I'd like to tell you about today's specials. We have a delicious chicken green salad sprinkled with walnuts and coated with a honey-glazed dressing. Next we have a Chicken Melody, baked to perfection. Please don't forget to try our Beef Burgundy over Noodles, one of my favorites."

Susan looked over at Barbara and said, "I'm leaning toward the salad; it sounds pretty good. What do you think?"

"Yes, please give us two of your salads. Could you give me an unsweetened ice tea with my order?"

"I'll have black coffee," Susan added.

A moment later, finding themselves alone, Susan turned to Barbara and asked "How is Rachel coping with her sister's disappearance?"

"Well, Rachel's attitude has changed significantly in the last week or so," Barbara said. "She loves the fact that I'm home and wishes it could be this way all the time."

The waitress soon returned with two glasses of water and

their drink orders. Taking a sip, Susan looked directly at her friend and cut to the chase.

"Okay, tell me. How are you and Mark holding up these days?"

Taken back by Susan's candor, Barbara explained. "Well, truthfully, much better than a few days ago when I announced I'd had enough of Mark's drinking as his way of coping with the abduction. I didn't appreciate his attitude. I was tired of fighting with him and doing everything on my own. I suggested if he wasn't happy, then he could leave. To bring the truth to him in a way he would understand, I walked over to the front door, opened it, and told him to get out."

"You did? Good for you!"

"Mark didn't know what to say. He stood in our entryway for several minutes, thinking. Then something within him must have snapped. Since that day he has quit his drinking and has been supportive in ways I never imagined."

"Just a minute, Barb. You're not the first wife who's dealt with a spouse's alcohol problem. My Johnny struggled with liquor. When John first joined the force, he and his buddies would spend most nights at the bars after work. At the time I was expecting our first child—one night when his partner arrived at our home smelling of booze. John appeared at the door and tried to kiss me goodbye. I was furious with him and took a swing at his head. Little did I know I would slip on my butt and would have to be rushed to the hospital because of it. Sadly, we lost the baby."

"I'm so sorry, Susan. You never told me."

"No, I wouldn't want you to feel ill toward John. After that incident John never went drinking with his pals again."

"I just never knew," Barbara remarked.

As they waited for their lunch to arrive, Susan asked, "So what's this news I hear about Rachel's school friend Jessica?"

"Rachel told you? I'm surprised," Barbara said. "Yes,

the other day when I picked her up from school, I noticed bruises on her arm and asked how she got them. She explained you were quite upset with her when you found out she had kept Jessica a secret."

"Yes, about that. This girl claims she saw Melissa's kidnappers."

"Really? Did she see their faces?"

"Unfortunately, we discovered it was all nothing but the vivid imagination of a young child. Or so it seems, according to Detective Reed. But he told me later something seemed odd. When Jessica answered his questions, she acted as if she had been coached on what to say to him.

"Jessica and Reed were completely alone in the living room of the house, while Jessica's parents remained outside on the porch, listening. After he completed his questioning, Jessica turned her head as if someone had called her name. Then she turned back again, looked into Reed's eyes, and let out a horrid laugh that was frightening."

Just then the food arrived. After a few moments Susan said, "I almost forgot to ask you: Whatever happened with that crystal light you found in your coat pocket?"

Barbara paused before taking another bite and replied, "The crystal! Yes, that's another story!"

"What do you mean?" Susan asked.

As Barbara told Susan the whole story of the night before, she listened intently, her mouth hanging open. She was unable to utter a word for a brief moment.

"I've never heard anything like that before!" Susan exclaimed, still in the grip of Barbara's story. Then she sat back in her chair and asked, "Where is the crystal now?"

"I left it on Melissa's dresser in her room where that demon thing appeared. I haven't had another incident since—at least from the spiritual world."

"Probably a good place to keep it, I would imagine.

Wow! That's something, a ghost haunting your home like that. Who would have guessed it possible?" Susan proclaimed.

"Susan, I haven't told Mark about this, and I would appreciate it if you wouldn't mention it either, okay?"

"Sure. Besides, who in the world would believe me anyway?" Susan replied. "Your secret is safe with me."

"Thank you. I don't want to sound like I'm going nutty, you understand."

"No one has to know."

"Hey, do you remember that Sterling character?"

"Sure, Barb, what about him?"

"Well, I finally met him. Yesterday—when I asked you to babysit Rachel after school."

"No! How on earth did you get his number?" Susan inquired.

"Well, that's another long story, something I'd rather not discuss at the moment. But I met Sterling in the city. It was a bit of a hassle, the stuff he put me through, but he's agreed to help me find Melissa after he finishes his latest case. He believes Melissa is alive. I think this darkness that visited me in Melissa's room is connected to her abduction."

"So Sterling believes Melissa's alive? I've never doubted it."

"Yes, if only we could find her soon. I feel she's still alive for some special purpose and that the reason for her staying alive will hopefully not come to an abrupt end."

"What do you mean?" Susan asked.

"Well, there's something else that has me puzzled. If Melissa is still alive, what do the hijackers want with her? There haven't been any ransom demands, which leaves me thinking Melissa was taken for some other reason. Especially now, after seeing that demon in her room—dark forces are at work in this."

"That's horrible!" Susan replied. "Why do you think that? Could it be this time of year? Maybe it has something to do with Halloween being just around the corner."

"I haven't a clue," Barbara said. "Well, if it's a fight they want, then I pray to the good Lord above that he arms me with the strength to bring the battle to their front door, not mine! Melissa is the innocent one who was taken in their diabolical plan. They'll regret taking my daughter—believe me! All that's needed is a break in the case. Then it'll all begin to make sense somehow and come crashing down on their heads, whoever they are.

"Time is slipping away, and I have begged Sterling to help me, but begging doesn't work in the spiritual world. He's involved with another case. A missing eight-year-old boy was kidnapped at the mall. Still, Sterling gave me his word that he will help us as soon as that case is solved. I'll feel a whole lot safer once he has. He can deal with those monsters lurking around; he's equipped to deal with such matters, not me."

After lunch they walked to Susan's car. "Well, I'd better get going myself. I have a ton of laundry still at home. John says he's running out of underwear; we don't want that to happen now, do we? John running around with a bare butt? Just imagine."

They both laughed. Still chuckling, Susan got in her SUV and drove away.

Chapter 16

After stopping by the grocery store, Barbara got in line at the school just as the bell sounded. She studied the children leaving Rachel's classroom and noticed Rachel talking to a girl she'd never seen before. Someone called Barbara's name; she turned and waved to the other mother, then turned back to look for Rachel. She was startled to see her daughter and her new friend standing by the car.

"Mom, this is Jessica. Can she come over?" Rachel asked.

Jessica stood listening to the conversation with considerable interest. "What did you say, Rachel?" Barbara replied, feeling awkward that they weren't alone.

"Is it all right if Jessica comes to our house to play?" Rachel again asked.

Momentarily at a loss for words—this was the girl who had bragged about seeing Melissa kidnapped, after all— Barbara mumbled, "Um," not knowing what else to say. Then she replied, "Maybe another time."

Jessica surprised them both by pleading, "Can I please come over, Mrs. Harding? We'll be as quiet as two little mice. I promise you won't hear us at all."

Then, turning to Rachel, she said, "Remember: We have a school project we're working on together that Miss Easton wants us to finish by this Friday."

"Is that true, Rachel?" Barbara asked.

"Yeah, Mom. Miss Easton wants us to make a cardboard cutout of our founding father's first outpost in the New World. Jessica said she would help me," Rachel answered.

Barbara didn't appreciate being put on the spot; she struggled with what to do. Finally, she agreed to allow this one visit to their home. "All right, get in and buckle your seat belts."

They hopped inside, and Barbara drove home. On the way Barbara informed Jessica she would have to call her mother to explain where she was.

"I already asked my mom if I could come over to your house after school to work on our project when she brought my lunch earlier,"

"You did?" Barbara replied, surprised by Jessica's answer. *How did this girl know I would agree to let her come to our house?* It seemed strange somehow.

Once they pulled into the driveway, Rachel and Jessica opened their car doors simultaneously, ran up to the house's front door, and waited patiently for Barbara to open the front door. Barbara, on the other hand, remained sitting in the driver's seat for a moment, watching the two girls play with one another, alert for any possible sign of something strange. But nothing out of the ordinary happened. The girls played tag like normal kids. After watching them for several minutes and not seeing anything unusual about Jessica, she decided perhaps the detective had been mistaken; she seemed like a normal kid her age.

Getting out of the car, Barbara continued to watch them chase each other on the front lawn and then tumble onto the grass. Seeing how the two played together, it felt good to see her daughter act like a kid again, considering what had happened to their family.

The girls entered the house and raced down the hall to Rachel's bedroom where they disappeared and went about building their school project. Barbara finished cleaning the kitchen; however, she began to feel something was wrong after a short time. Unsure what it could be, she washed the soap from her hands and dried them on a towel.

Looking down the hall toward Rachel's room, all was quiet; she could no longer hear laughter coming from the bedroom so she hurried down the hallway.

She called out to Rachel and heard no reply. But as she passed by Melissa's bedroom, she noticed no light was shining from the crystal—in fact, the small object no longer sat on the dresser. Gripped by a new fear, she stared out the bedroom window toward the street, wondering what she was going to do now that her only protection from the monsters was gone. Suddenly, she heard the front door open. She looked out and saw Jessica making her escape from the house.

Barbara dashed outside and ran after her daughter's friend. Jessica turned and saw Barbara—the race was on. Barbara quickly overtook the child and caught her just as she ran across the neighbor's lawn. She pounced on her as if she were a lioness catching a small gazelle.

"Give it to me now!" Barbara ordered.

"Give you what?" Jessica screamed while struggling to break free.

Looking down at the girl's fist, she saw a familiar blue bath towel in her hand. She began to pry it free from her fingers. Jessica struggled to get away but couldn't match Barbara's tenacity and strength. Gradually, her tiny fingers were pried open, exposing the crystal.

It no longer shined; it looked as if all its life had been drained away. It was no more than a dark, lifeless orb, a black stone that radiated no light. As they continued to struggle for ownership of the crystal, Jessica's voice altered to a low growl.

"Let go, bitch!"

The girl punched Barbara in the face, sending her head reeling backward. Stars floated all around, and her vision blurred as she struggled to come back to reality and not let go of the little girl's hand. She could taste blood from her split lip.

"Is that all you got?" Barbara shouted. Feeling a new resolve, she gripped Jessica's fingers and pried them apart, refusing to accept anything but the prize that lay within the girl's grasp.

The crystal and towel slipped free from Jessica's grip and fell to the grass a second later. With lightning-fast reflexes, Barbara grabbed it; a slight glow reappeared from the deepest recesses of the darkness inside it. Its broadening brightness came alive as Barbara held it aloft. The power Jessica demonstrated had weakened, and she looked up at Barbara as if pleading to be released from whatever it was that held her prisoner.

The sun's rays hit the crystal, and a brilliant light shot out in many directions until multiple beams intersected, forming a dome-like shape overhead that covered them. The light shining from the sun intensified the covering, and soon translucent shades of red, blue, and orange radiated from above.

Protected from the worldly influences of evil, inside the beautiful and brilliant golden-jeweled dome, rays of light bounced about until one hit Jessica, followed rapidly by another and another. Soon myriad rays penetrated her body. Jessica stood in silence, her eyes closed. Unaware of what was happening, darkness began to flow out of her.

Suddenly, a spot of black oozing goo formed and took shape, much like a raven, outside Jessica's body. The powers of the dome struggled to free Jessica from her unwanted parasite. Next a pocket developed through the wall. Released from Jessica's body, the raven-like creature was pushed outside the dome through a small opening the size of a quarter.

With the ejection of the black raven from the dome of light, the small opening closed tightly. Try as it might, the birdlike creature couldn't penetrate the hard shell. All it could do was screech at them from outside the dome. Whatever it was, it was desperate to enter the young girl once more.

Its beak pecked at the lit surface while its little red eyes turned every which way, searching for a way back inside. It let out another screech that attracted other black crows from the nearby trees.

As the other birds approached, the spirit raven flew directly toward them and, in midair one by one, gripped its talons deep into their bodies. Then it breathed into its victims, emitting blackness that covered their tiny forms. The demonic-possessed birds attacked the dome a moment later, trying to get inside its jeweled arc of light, but with no success.

Looking at Jessica, Barbara saw the brightly colored beams bouncing in and out of her body, searching for any remaining evil within. The crystal's rays bounced about inside the dome. The process was beautiful to watch and made Barbara feel safe. The light was soft and warm and wasn't to be feared. It grew brighter, increasing in intensity until it was so bright Barbara could hardly look at it. As she continued holding the crystal, she instinctively knew what to do and brought it closer to Jessica's body while keeping hold of her so she couldn't get away.

Barbara began to see a change in Jessica's appearance. The darkness that shrouded the child started to escape outward from her body. A dark, oily-looking goo floated just above their heads, and a golden lining began to encapsulate it. The sludge hung in the air while tiny lightning bolts of energy exploded within its new cocoon and soon destroyed it.

Outside the dome of light, the spirit raven, ignoring all the other birds that worked tirelessly at penetrating the exterior of the crown, flew and landed on the outside of the dome, screeching loudly and looking about with tiny dark red eyes filled with hostile intent.

It let out another loud screech before flapping its broad wings and flying away. The other birds stopped pecking at the dome and dropped dead onto the lawn.

Preoccupied with the crows, Barbara had forgotten about Jessica, and she turned to look at her. The young girl, with terror-filled eyes, began to cry and sob, free of the evil that had held her captive. Relaxing her grip, Barbara saw only a frightened girl who desperately wanted to get away. At that moment, as if moved by a will stronger than herself, the overhead dome faded.

Barbara let go of her grip, turned to the girl, and quickly asked, "How do you feel, Jessica?"

Suddenly free and aware of her surroundings, a frightened Jessica ran away. All around Barbara were dead birds. Then, by accident, Barbara stepped on one, crushing it beneath her feet; black smoke puffed outward from its body, and it dissolved from her sight, back down into the ground below, leaving an oily residue behind in the grass.

The rest of the birds dissolved as if on cue, leaving only a greasy sign of their existence behind. Barbara felt relieved that once again she had been able to wreak havoc on the plans of some master evil. *But why am I in the middle of it all?* she asked herself. *Is there something more to this evil than meets the eye? And how is it all connected?* The crystal again flowed with a mysterious energy.

Barbara realized she was standing on her neighbor's front lawn. Feeling as if someone was watching her, she turned and saw Mrs. Andersen staring back at her from her living room window.

Not knowing what else to do, Barbara smiled and waved to her neighbor. She knew no one would believe Mrs. Andersen, even if she told the world what had just happened on her lawn. Frankly, Barbara wouldn't have believed it herself if it hadn't just happened to her.

As Barbara entered her home, a bewildered Rachel came running to ask her mother where Jessica was. Rachel explained she had gone to get her a glass of water, and when she'd come back to her bedroom, Jessica had left. Barbara calmly said Jessica had to run home to be with her mother. She'd probably been missing for some time.

"Oh!" Rachel answered, not grasping the meaning of what her mother had just said.

Barbara watched the crystal continue to radiate light from her hand as she held it tightly.

Seeing it, Rachel exclaimed, "Look! You fixed it!"

"Fixed what?" Barbara asked.

"Oh, the nightlight Jessica kept staring at," Rachel replied.

"She was?" Barbara asked.

"Yes, Mom. She saw it in Melissa's bedroom and asked me what was shining so brightly. I said it was a new nightlight you had bought at the store. She was wondering why it shined so much in the daylight and wanted to look at it more closely. She asked me to get it for her. So I did.

"After I took the crystal thing from the dresser, Jessica said she didn't want to hold it. For some reason it scared her. Afterward, she asked me to get her a towel.

I had to go to the bathroom. When I came back to my

room and gave her the blue towel, she told me she was thirsty and asked for a glass of water. When I came back from the kitchen, she was gone. I looked all over the house, and then I saw you outside on Mrs. Andersen's lawn."

"I get it—now," Barbara answered.

After they had walked back into the house, she hugged Rachel and said, "Now go to your room and finish your homework."

"All right, Mom," Rachel replied and ran back toward her bedroom.

Barbara walked into Melissa's room and set the crystal back on top of the dresser. As she walked away she noticed the small object showering the room in a protective brilliance, much like a searchlight on a rocky shoreline warning ships of the danger. Walking into the kitchen, she decided to call Susan while she prepared dinner.

"Susan, it's Barb. You can't believe what just happened!"

"What! Tell me."

"Do you remember Jessica, Rachel's friend at school?"

"Yes, of course. How could I forget?"

"Well, listen carefully, something strange happened today after I picked up Rachel from school,"

Barbara described the events of the afternoon; however, partway through her story, Susan stopped her.

"Wait a minute! John and I are coming over. I need to hear this in person!"

"Ok, I'll explain more when I see you. Oh, Susan, I didn't want to disturb your plans this evening," she announced, apologizing.

"Don't worry about it. We haven't decided yet what we're going to do for dinner; John likes Chinese food, I want Italian. We're coming over as soon as I get changed."

"Well, could you do me a big favor? I'm cooking a stew

for dinner, and you both are welcome to stay. I always make too much, anyway,"

"That sounds lovely. I'll tell John to hurry up. We're coming to the Hardings' house for dinner instead,"

"If you wouldn't mind, could you pick up some sourdough bread on the way over?"

"Yes, no worries. I already bought some for when I make John spaghetti. See ya soon. Bye."

When Mark walked through the door, he instantly smelled the stew cooking on the stove and shouted out to Barbara, asking what they were having for dinner.

"Stew."

"My favorite!" he remarked.

"John and Susan are coming over for dinner tonight."

"They are?" Mark asked, surprised. "What's the occasion?"

"Well, I have something I want to discuss with Susan that would probably bore you to tears."

"Oh, I get it. Girl talk."

"Yes, you could call it that," Barbara replied. "They'll be here soon so get cleaned up."

"Sure thing."

Mark walked over to plant a kiss on her lips. For the first time he saw her swollen lip and quickly asked, "What in the hell happened to you?"

"Oh, that. I can explain it."

Before she could explain they heard pounding on their front door.

Barbara turned to Mark and asked, "Who on earth could that be?"

"I haven't a clue," he responded and went to see who it was.

To his surprise when he opened the front door, he was confronted with a haggard-looking brunette who appeared to be in her late thirties. She wore holey blue jeans and a black rocker T-shirt. A lit cigarette hung from her mouth. Seeing this hostile stranger standing there, Mark thought she must have the wrong address.

"Can I help you?" he asked.

"Yes!" she screamed back. "Where is that bitch wife of yours? I have something to say to her."

"Pardon me, lady. What did you call my wife?"

"A bitch is what I said! Now where is she?"

Mark was unsure of what to do, but Barbara appeared at the front door before he could make a decision.

"Yes, may I help you?" Barbara inquired. She was annoyed at the stranger for using foul language in case Rachel overheard.

"Yes, you sure the hell can," she answered with smoke from her cigarette flowing out her nostrils. "My name is Eileen Taylor, and I want to ask you what in the hell gives you the right to abuse my little girl, Jessica!"

"Jessica?" Barbara asked in surprise, having never seen the woman before.

The woman turned around and pointed to a rusty old blue station wagon parked along the curb, which Barbara hadn't noticed until now. Sitting in the passenger seat was Jessica in tears, staring back.

"Well, about that, I want to explain if you'd let me—" Barbara said but was quickly cut off by the angry mother.

"Let you explain what?" the woman screamed. Next she turned and yelled for Jessica to come. When she arrived at the door, the frazzled mother ordered her to come closer. She gripped her by a lock of hair and shouted, "Look, try to explain this if you can!"

She lifted the sleeve of Jessica's dress, revealing a large black bruise that covered her forearm.

"Oh, my goodness!" Barbara responded while holding

her hand over her mouth. "That's terrible!" she cried, looking over at Mark as if he had an explanation. "I had no idea that when I gripped her arm I hurt her that badly."

"Well, you did!" the mother shouted, still upset.

"I'm so sorry again. But you should know I caught your daughter trying to steal something of great value from my home, and she gave me this cut on my lip when I tried to take back what she stole from us."

Eileen looked at Barbara's mouth, which still looked swollen, dark, and bloody, and replied, "Well, it looks to me like you should know better than to abuse a child. I even had to miss work down at the Wild Moose Bar, thanks to you!"

Turning to her defenseless daughter, Eileen abruptly yelled out, "Is it true you tried to steal something from these people's house, you little brat?" She held up her hand, about to strike her across the face as Jessica braced herself for the impact.

Mark grabbed the mother's hand, stopping her before she was able to swing, and responded, "That's enough, lady. You made your point. Now leave her alone. I think you should be on your way before things get ugly."

"They're already ugly, buddy!" Eileen screamed. "I'm going to go to the police department to file a complaint of child abuse on your wife!"

At that moment John and Susan arrived. After hearing all the commotion, they parked in the driveway and walked over to the front door.

"There are other ways to handle a kleptomaniac!" Eileen shouted and repeated her declaration that she was going to the authorities to file a complaint against Barbara.

Having heard enough of the woman's babbling, Susan became angry and shouted, "Go right ahead, lady, but there's something perhaps you might want to consider. My husband, John, is a retired U.S. Marshal. Why not file a complaint with him?" she said smugly.

The angry woman quickly got herself under control. She turned back to Jessica and yelled at her to get back in the car. Jessica dashed toward her mother's station wagon, jumped inside, slammed the car door shut, and waited for her mom to arrive, knowing some punishment was awaiting her once she got home.

"This isn't over!" Eileen said as she angrily returned to her car, leaving a trail of cigarette smoke behind.

Once she got inside the old clunker and started it up, a dark cloud blew out its tailpipe. She stepped on the accelerator, making the rear tires squeal under the engine's torque, and sped away, leaving behind a dense, dark cloud of exhaust.

In a funny voice John turned around and said, "I would hate to be the guy who has to buy her tires each week!"

Everyone broke out in laughter, but John stopped laughing once he noticed Barbara's swollen lip. "What happened to your lip?"

"It's nothing. Just a little cut is all," Barbara replied.

"That little brat Jessica hit Barbara in the mouth when she caught her stealing something from our house," Mark snapped.

"Now what's this Jessica stuff all about?" Susan asked, curious about Barbara's cut lip and what she was trying to say on the phone.

Since they still had a little time before dinner, Barbara announced, "You boys go in the house. I want to show Susan my neighbor's rose garden. We'll be right back."

"Sure, that's fine," Mark replied. "John, did you see that article about the baseball player's salary cap on the sports page?"

Barbara grabbed Susan by the arm and said, "Let me show you."

Walking over to Mrs. Andersen's front lawn, Barbara pointed to an oily spot in the grass and asked, "Do you see that?"

Susan looked down at the grass and replied, "See what?"

"Don't you see it?"

Looking down again at the lawn, Susan responded, "Not really. I'm not sure exactly what you're talking about here. All I see is a blackish spot that looks like someone dumped a little motor oil on the ground."

"You're looking at the remnants of what used to be inside some blackbirds and young Jessica." said Barbara.

"What do you mean—someone filled Jessica up with motor oil?"

"Listen, that blackish spot was some creature that crawled out of Jessica and controlled a group of birds. When it was defeated, it flew away, leaving behind the dead birds on the ground. I accidentally smashed one with my foot, and the air blew out of it like a balloon popping, and then it dissolved and soaked into the ground along with the rest of the birds—sending them straight to hell, I hope."

"Barbara," Susan sounded very concerned, "maybe you're under too much stress, and your mind is playing tricks on you."

"Jessica was under some spell. She had to have been. Something or someone so powerful, with an evil voice, spoke through her, calling me a bitch," Barbara responded.

"Barbara, I'm thinking you're hallucinating."

Just then the front door opened and out walked Mrs. Andersen. She wore a red housecoat covering her round body, and her gray hair hung to her shoulders. She walked up to Barbara, reached out her hand, and took hold of it.

"I saw it all! I was astounded when I saw that little girl smack you in the mouth. But afterward, hearing the man's voice call you a bitch! Plus the light! Oh my, the light, with its beautiful spectrum, and the blackish goo coming out of the little girl—well, I couldn't believe what I was seeing. I want you to know it scared me half to death. I was never more grateful to have you as a neighbor than when I saw you save her," she explained, still in shock.

"Thank you. It means a lot to me," Barbara replied.

"Well, enough of this business," said Susan. "I think it's time to focus on Melissa now. Damn if we don't find that child."

"I know," Barbara agreed. "Let's get back home. I'm sure the boys are half-starved by now; besides, I'm getting hungry, too."

Looking at her neighbor, Barbara asked, "Would you care to join us for dinner?"

"I would," she said, "but my Henry will be home soon enough, and I'm sure he'll want me to fix him something for supper. Thanks anyway," she responded, then waved goodbye and returned home.

Chapter 17

Sterling agreed to meet his old friend Jack at his favorite secluded coastal restaurant on a narrow beach overlooking the bay just outside of New York City.

The waitress brought Jack a cold beer. He thanked her, turned to Sterling, and said, "What's on your mind? Tell me the real reason for calling me down here besides buying me that beer you always promised me."

"I'm about to embark on another case that I know nothing about, but I sense it's perilous and somehow involves some ancient evil connection to the Hardings' missing daughter."

"Oh! You decided to take the case after all—after you jumped my ass for her calling you," Jack replied, sipping his beer.

"You knew I would be pissed off so don't act so surprised. True friendship means understanding one another, and I only jumped your ass, as you put it, because I was intensely working to solve this other case."

"Yeah, right," Jack laughed.

"That's the truth, Jack. You must believe me. Now that the missing boy case has been solved, I only wish the outcome had been better. But here's where things are different from that case, Jack. The Harding girl is still alive."

"She is?" Jack replied, sounding surprised. After taking

another sip from his bottle, he said, "How do you know this, Sterling? Oh, never mind. I can already guess. You had a vision, right?"

"Jack, if I didn't know any better, I would say you don't believe," Sterling joked.

"I do feel things—you know that. Ever since I pulled you from that car crash when you were a youngster, I have recognized your gifts and abilities and supported your endeavors to find missing persons. But just to let you know, I met with the Hardings' friend John, who used to work down at the U.S. Marshals office."

"A U.S. Marshal, you say—someone who can help us in our search for the missing child." Looking away momentarily, he admitted the evidence had him worried. "In a vision I had there some terrible dark and ancient force lurking in the shadows, ready to strike if anyone got in its way."

"Kid, you know I've got your back, and I always will. Just be safe out there, okay? You can't do this all alone."

"This Barbara Harding has the fight needed to find her missing daughter," Sterling said. "There will be no giving up. After seeing her willingness to stand her ground, I believe she won't break but will win this." He paused for a moment. "Giving her the Mother's Regret crystal was the right choice. Evil surrounds her, growing darkness that somehow involves Melissa, though I'm unable to understand what it is."

"What in the world is the Mother's Regret crystal?" Jack asked.

"It's something powerful that's used to ward off evil. I first saw this darkness in a vision about two months ago when I was sick with the flu. As I lay in bed, slipping in and out of sleep, my body was no use to me whatsoever.

"As my mortal being was busy waging war on the flu

virus, I…oh wait. Speaking of Barbara Harding, there she is now," Sterling announced. He stood and waved her over to their table.

As Barbara approached she noticed Jack still seemed upset that she had stolen Sterling's number without his permission. He just nodded shortly at her and nursed his cold beer.

Sterling waved for the waitress to come over to their table. Taking his seat next to Barbara, he said, "No matter. I'm just glad to see you made it."

The waitress appeared and asked Barbara if she wished to order something to drink.

"Yes, thank you, I'll have a glass of Cabernet Sauvignon."

Turning back to Sterling, she said, "Please continue."

"I had a vision about two months ago while I was sick with the flu. While I slept late one afternoon, I began to dream; my revelation started simply enough. I was overlooking a grass meadow, watching the tall stalks blowing in the wind. It was as peaceful as a spring day and just as harmless.

"Walking through the tall grass, the sky began to turn dark. Eventually, the path led to a high cliff. Hearing crashing waves below me, I stopped dead in my tracks; I didn't move, not wanting to fall to the rocks below.

"As I stood near the cliff's edge, I heard what sounded like a woman crying down below, near the shore. Getting down on my knees, I crawled to the edge and looked over the cliff. There I saw a woman chained to a rocky outcropping of boulders in the surf. I watched helplessly from a distance as she pleaded for my help.

"As I continued to watch, her predicament changed; the tide began coming in. Waves began to crash against the back of the boulders, sending water flowing down around her.

Seeing the desperation on her face as the waves continued hammering the shoreline, I knew I couldn't reach her in time to free her.

"She was too far offshore; she would drown in the surf. I watched from the safety of the tall cliff; I noticed a dark and menacing figure approaching a distance away, camouflaged against the black sky. As I stared into the darkness, I saw a pair of large, flapping wings holding a beast aloft, bringing it ever closer. Looking down at the surf, I could see the water level continuing to rise; the woman's feet were now fully covered by the cold, dark water. As for the flying beast, I made out its shape among the dark clouds and knew right away it was a dragon with a spiked head and a massive body.

"As it flew through the air, the dragon searched for something desperately. Soon it discovered what it desired most—the powerless woman locked in chains.

"Slowing itself, it flapped its wings to brace for a landing. The dark nails gripped the top of a giant boulder as it rested its massive body. The dragon's heavily plated black scales glistened in the fullness of the moon; they covered its entire body from its breast up to its spiked head and looked as hard as iron. Its eyelids were narrow slits that covered dark orange orbs, shielded with thick plates layered to protect its eyes.

"It lifted its head into the night sky and emitted a ball of fire that completely lit up the surrounding shoreline, making everything bright. It had found what it had been searching for; it lowered its large, spiky head and opened its great mouth, exposing razor-sharp teeth. I felt sorrow for the woman who was about to be devoured by the horrible dragon.

"But at that moment from the eastern sky I noticed a small cluster of lights rapidly approaching the shoreline. As I stared in that direction, a fierce wind began to blow around me. It lifted me completely off my feet. I became weightless and floated above the cliffs and rocky shoreline. The light from the east drew closer and caught the attention of the dragon. Without warning several small lights in the shape of small crystals surrounded me. They reminded me of little stars that twinkled and flashed as if alive."

Just then the waitress walked up with the glass of wine on her small tray. Setting it down on the table in front of Barbara, she asked if anyone wanted anything else.

"What the hell? I'm off duty as of ten minutes ago. I'll take another beer for my friend and me," Jack said.

"Is that all?" the waitress asked.

"No! Tell me, do you guys still serve those little crab cakes?"

"Yes, they're our house specialty." The server smiled brightly.

"Good. I'll take two orders."

Then he turned to Sterling and said, "I'm telling you, you have to try those little crab cakes. Damn, they're good." A few moments later after receiving his second beer, he apologized for the interruption and said, "Please continue."

Sterling adjusted himself in his seat and said, "Now where was I? Oh yes, the bright stars. I then found myself lowered to the sandy shoreline. In some mysterious way I had a part to play in this drama. My attention was drawn to the opposite side of the beach; a white stallion ran toward me.

"The dragon wasn't happy about being interrupted by annoying lights or the appearance of me and the stallion. It lifted its enormous head, stretched out its neck, and stared hatefully at us. It let out a flame of fire that, thankfully, was too far away to harm me.

"Flapping its wings, it lifted its massive body upward and flew toward me. Fortunately, the stallion arrived first. I jumped on its saddle and galloped away from the horrible beast.

"The steed felt unbridled hatred toward the dragon, and I realized the monster had to be destroyed at all cost.

"But how? The stallion, to my surprise, galloped directly toward the flying monster, and then a cluster of stars appeared around me again. They seemed to focus all their light on a small object that hung around the horse's neck. As I looked down I saw a key and small crystal hanging from the chain.

"I knew I had seen that object before; I just didn't know where. Regardless, I knew I couldn't allow the dragon to kill that woman. The small crystal had to be the key. Desperately, I reached down and ripped the two items from the chain. As the dragon made a diving pass to destroy us with its massive paws, the stallion made a quick turn, avoiding certain death.

"I rode the horse toward the shoreline, avoiding one near miss after another from the dragon, which became frustrated at its failed attempts. The stallion was too nimble and quick. Though its size and strength were far superior to ours, the dragon couldn't make the necessary turns as quickly as we could. Each time it narrowly missed us the rushing air from its massive body practically knocked me off the horse. However, I remained steadfast in my resolve to reach the woman chained to the rock.

"Eventually, I reached the rocky shoreline and jumped off the horse, taking with me the key and crystal. I ran between the boulders into the pounding surf, struggling to reach the woman. When I arrived the water was up to my waist, and I fought to get to her in time. My teeth chattered from the cold as crashing waves hit my body, hindering my advance.

"At that moment the dragon landed in the pounding surf, and I found myself having to avoid its snapping jaws and sharp teeth as it attempted to catch me in its gaping mouth. Finally, I reached the rock that held the woman prisoner. She looked at me with pleading eyes as I hurried to unlock the chains that bound her. As I fumbled with the locks, she begged me to hurry because the dragon was almost upon us.

"I unlatched the chains, releasing the woman from her imprisonment. I still held the small crystal within my other hand, which had come to life with blinding light.

"But just then I felt the hot breath of the dragon on the back of my neck. When I turned around there was his great mouth, wide open, ready to devour us both. I knew we were about to die, and I looked with compassion upon the woman whom I had just set free. Contritely, I handed the crystal object to her and prepared myself for death.

"The crystal within her hand came alive and filled the darkness around us with blinding light. As the brightness intensified the dragon began to moan in pain. It lifted its head into the sky and let out a blast of fire. Everything around us changed, and the dragon writhed in torment from the shining light. What happened next astonished me. The woman somehow knew what to do, and as I watched she attacked the dragon. Holding the bright crystal object, she shoved it into the dragon's chest.

"The light from the crystal penetrated the dragon's scales, causing them to become transparent. I could see the large red pounding heart within the chest of the beast. The light's brightness began to melt away the animal's skin, and the crystal started to smoke as if it was on fire.

"The exposed heart of the dragon made the woman more determined to kill the creature. The raw power of the crystal she gripped tightly in her hand caused her arm to shudder as she pressed it into the dragon's chest cavity. She almost lost her grip and dropped the small object into the surf. The energy that flowed from the crystal was intensely powerful.

Now joined with a particular element that wasn't obvious to me at the time, the two factors were an unstoppable force.

"The dragon's heart was now unprotected, vulnerable to attack. The woman removed a small dagger from the crevice of the rock behind her, which I hadn't noticed before, and plunged it deep into the dragon's heart. Burning red blood poured out into the dark water. It let out an enormous, bellowing cry, collapsed backward into the pounding waves, and died.

"The woman, whom I had never seen before, turned to me and announced, 'You see, I slew the evil. Now it needs to release my daughter.'

"After I awoke from my vision back in my bed, dripping wet, I pondered what she'd meant by that statement. I realized I had seen that small crystal before; it was somewhere in my collection of mysterious artifacts collected over the years. Rising from my bed, I felt light-headed as I walked into my study.

"I rummaged through the drawers in my antique armoire. Finally, in the back of one of the drawers under an old book, I found the crystal. It was nothing more than a trinket, a tiny inanimate object I hadn't considered anything more than costume jewelry.

"When I saw it in the drawer, it looked different. Something I had never noticed before was coming from within its crystalline body: a small light that shone at its core as if it had batteries. But it didn't come with batteries; of that I was sure."

Barbara let out a gasp as she recognized the crystal she had found in her pocket, but Sterling took no notice and continued his story.

"I inherited the crystal about seven years ago from a client named Penny Martin. She told me it was supposed to have some magical power that would help me find lost children, but it was worthless; it hadn't helped her find her missing daughter. She seemed grateful to be rid of it. The previous owner had confessed to Penny over thirty years earlier that it was an imposing force to those whom it chose to help. After Penny had given it to me, she admitted she had stolen it from her friend Betty Rochelle.

"You see, Penny had stayed overnight at Betty's house and accidentally found her friend's diary open and unlocked under her bed. She read about her boyfriend, Brian, and Betty secretly meeting behind her back. That night Penny and her friend got into a terrible fight over the loss of Penny's true love. If not for being betrayed, Penny would have never done the unthinkable; she wasn't the type of person to take things that weren't hers.

"Penny knew the family placed great value on this small crystal object and that if she took it, the family would be upset. If they found out Betty's friend was the culprit, that would certainly get her friend in trouble. Within a few days of Penny returning home Betty disappeared. They searched everywhere for her, but she vanished without a trace. Did the crystal keep the family safe from evil? Penny was left asking that question.

"When I held the object in my hand, I felt something indescribable. It possessed an energy that was lying dormant and waiting for the particular key that would release its power.

"Then a long time later, after I had the vision of the woman fighting the darkness disguised as a dragon, I knew it wasn't mine to keep so I waited for the right owner to appear. When I heard Barbara on the phone, pleading for my help, I knew I wasn't going to be able to come to her aid right away, and yet it wasn't until I heard Barbara say the words— 'You see, I slew the evil. Now it needs to release my daughter'—that I realized the crystal was destined for her.

She has the power to wield it; fate will prove me right."

"I'm still not sure why I said that," Barbara announced.

Jack responded, "Look, kid, I don't know about all of this mumbo-jumbo witchcraft stuff, but I have worked as a detective long enough to see what evil can do. I'm not talking about the evil of another time or dimension. I can't afford to; I have too much on my plate as it is. I'll be there if you need me. But, Sterling, if you come across any evidence concerning Mrs. Harding's missing daughter, you have to tell me at once."

Sterling laughed slightly at his friend's seriousness and said, "Listen, Jack, you know I would never keep any evidence from you. Come on, how long have we known each other?"

After taking another sip from his beer, Jack replied, "A long time, kid, but truthfully, there's been times I didn't hear about the criminals until after you kicked the shit out of them."

Sterling laughed and responded, "I know, Jack. You got me there, old friend, but this is different. I believe the villain in this story is from another time or century, not some creep who lives with his mother and is troubled because he couldn't feel whole without taking a hostage. Not this time! Everything that surrounds this abduction points to something unimaginable, something that has taken residence at Barbara's house."

Barbara jumped in and said, "Yes, that's correct. How do you know that, Sterling? I haven't told you about my experience at my home or the evil creature that tried to attack me."

"Last night I had a vision, a view into the dark world of some unknown villain who's invaded your home, Barbara. Because of this I sought out a powerful sorcerer named Stannis. I hate to admit this, but I'm completely out of my league when it comes to powerful magic!"

"Well, can you at least tell me about the vision you had?" Barbara inquired.

Jack, finishing his beer, said, "Yes, I'll listen, but that doesn't make me a believer in that mumbo jumbo."

"If you both insist," Sterling replied and began to explain what he'd seen in his vision.

"I was at your house, Barbara. I saw your living room, with the brightly colored flower-printed couch and an antique piano near the front door, in front of your living room window. You have a bookshelf with books and movies combined, stacked onto one another on the opposite wall."

Drinking her wine, Barbara became intrigued by his detailed description of her home and listened as he went through each room, explaining what he had seen.

Sterling described details unique to Melissa's bedroom as if he had been there recently. Inside the bedroom he'd seen various teen idol posters hanging on the walls, a picture of the family on her dresser, and stuffed animals on her bed. He even described Melissa's favorite animal.

Something present in Melissa's room troubled Sterling. He turned to Barbara.

"A source of great evil has been granted passage into your home. Listen to me: Do not remove that crystal. Without it I fear you will have no protection from this evil or its purpose for being there."

"Great! What does that mean?" Barbara asked, desperate to learn more.

Jack suggested he come to Barbara's house and arrest the intruder.

Sterling laughed at the idea, explaining the evil he talked about wasn't a criminal. He warned both of them that if they were to see such a monster alive, it would frighten them so severely that they would be frozen with fear and not able to run away.

Barbara answered, "I have already seen this creature. The crystal saved me from his attacks, keeping the monster at bay. Can you tell me, Sterling, why this is happening to my family?"

"I don't have the answers you seek. For this I must meet up with someone stronger than myself to learn the solutions to those questions. To do this I have to leave now.

"I'm confident no harm will come to your family as long as the crystal is kept in the house, close to where you saw the evil trying to enter. Something invited the darkness into your home, and it'll take something powerful to remove it."

Barbara, after taking another sip, turned to Sterling. "I have to tell you something else that happened. There's a girl named Jessica who I believe was possessed by this evil that you speak of. She tried to steal the crystal from my house. What would cause someone so innocent to perform such a brave act of thievery?"

Jack downed his last remaining beer and said, "Hey, I have to be going. I have things to take care of at home. Hey, kid, take care of yourself, okay?" He stood and began to walk away.

"I will, Jack. You can count on that."

Swallowing his last sip of beer and standing up, Sterling left a twenty-dollar bill on the table. Turning to Barbara, he asked, "Are you ready to go?"

"Yes, thank you," she responded.

By the time Barbara and Sterling left the small restaurant they noticed Jack pulling away in his car.

"Good old, Jack. I don't know what I've had done without him on my side," Sterling announced.

"Yes, you two seem to have a friendship that extends beyond ordinary relationships, as though he's a father figure in some ways."

"I suppose you're right, but at times we both drive each other crazy," Sterling admitted, laughing.

"I have to confess having some evil camping out at my home is somewhat scary."

"I understand. Please listen to me for just a moment. I didn't feel like saying anything to Jack, the unbeliever; he wouldn't understand. Sometime soon you're going to be visited by someone, a traitor to the cause, who will explain to you the reason for your daughter's abduction. That's all I can say for now. I really must be going."

"At least let me ask you this: Who's this Stannis character you spoke of?"

"Sometime ago I had the pleasure of meeting a conjurer of magic. Sadly, it didn't end well. I'm not sure he'll aid us in our fight, but I have to try."

"Thank you, Sterling, if for nothing else then for giving me the crystal. I don't know what I would have done that night the creature came at me if I didn't have it."

"Well, we don't want to think of that. Listen, I'll be in contact, I promise, but I really must go."

"Thank you, Sterling," Quickly reaching out, Barbara wrapped her arms around the stranger and hugged him tightly.

Afterward, Barbara watched Sterling drive away. She hoped they would meet again; sadly, all would be lost if not. She returned home while Sterling drove off to see Stannis, the sorcerer who was more experienced dealing with this type of threat—a dangerous evil that had moved into their happy home, and one she would face alone if ever she hoped to see her daughter again.

Chapter 18

Barbara sat at the kitchen table paying bills. It was still dark on this early morning, and the kitchen light gave off a comforting glow. But the comfort of the kitchen couldn't hide the facts. It was becoming painfully evident she would soon have to return to work. Yes, the company had given her leave with pay, but that would quickly come to an end. And although she had been on leave for only a short time, her recent experiences had been so intense it felt like a lifetime. She needed Sterling.

When he asked me if I was willing to do whatever it took to find my daughter, I never imagined evil spirits. How did he know something evil was here in my house? What did he see in me that I didn't see myself? She pondered these questions as she busily chewed the end of her pencil.

At that moment Buster began barking wildly to get outside. After opening the blinds and the sliding door, Barbara was almost knocked to the ground as Buster dashed toward their old boat parked in the yard and stood at attention by the trailer's rear axle. He was barking continuously and refused to settle down.

Hmm, what's got you so agitated, dog? Barbara looked around but saw nothing out of the ordinary. She grabbed the rechargeable flashlight they kept plugged into the wall socket, flicked it on, and went out to check on Buster.

Barbara shined the light inside the boat. To her amazement, hunkered down under several life jackets, sat a familiar-looking teenage girl. The girl was close to Melissa's age. She had long, flowing blonde hair and wore dirty blue jeans and a rain jacket. On her feet were muddy boots. She looked as if she had been sleeping outdoors.

The young girl stood up and announced, "You're the Bishop mother, aren't you?"

"Pardon me?" Barbara replied, studying the intruder. "Do I know you?"

"You're Melissa's mother," the girl responded.

"That's right. But who are you, and what are you doing sleeping in our boat?"

"My name is Heather Taylor; I've been sleeping here for the past two nights," she said apologetically. "I didn't think you would mind."

Feeling put on the spot, Barbara asked, "What exactly do you want? Tell me, or else I'll call the police on you for trespassing."

"I want to save my father."

"What does that have to do with me?"

"I want to save my father; he's a good man."

"Okay, but what does that have to do with me?" Barbara repeated.

"Because your daughter is the one my father has to sacrifice. Then he'll be able to keep my family safe."

"What the hell are you saying? Is my daughter to be sacrificed to keep your family safe? That doesn't make sense. I don't know you or your family!"

The girl stood there, unwilling to budge. She stomped her feet on the hardwood floor of the boat. "If he sacrifices the innocent, my father will be forever lost to the evil darkness. I must stop this before it happens."

Pausing for a moment Barbara reevaluated. *None of what this girl says makes any sense.* But she had seen enough recently that made her want to hear more. "Wait here. I'll be back in a minute."

In the house she grabbed the crystal, hid it in her pants pocket, and returned. As she got near the girl again, the crystal remained inert. "Come inside the house."

Heather nodded and wiped the tears from her eyes. Crawling out the back of the boat, she stood next to Barbara with her backpack in her hand. Buster licked the new guest's hand repeatedly, and Heather giggled.

Walking into the kitchen, Barbara turned to Heather. "I've already had run-ins with your younger sister, Jessica, and your stepmother, and now you. This is becoming stranger by the minute." Unsure what else to say, Barbara asked, "Is there anyone you want me to call? You must have family who is worried sick."

"No, none of them can ever know I'm here," Heather replied. She turned to the glass patio slider, locked it tightly, and pulled the vertical blinds closed behind her.

"Now you're making me nervous," Barbara said.

"You should be nervous. I know I would be if I were you."

"What is all this about Melissa's sacrifice? Do you know where my daughter is?" Barbara said, trying to maintain her composure.

"I don't know where she is now. I believe my father was keeping her in an abandoned house for a while."

Barbara wanted to pounce on the girl and beat the truth out of her but knew she had to keep her calm. She asked Heather to have a seat at the kitchen table and inquired if she wanted some breakfast.

"Yes, I'm starving," Heather responded.

Barbara had cooked some home-fried potatoes earlier.

The skillet was still warm, and it only took a moment to fry up eggs. After bringing her a plate and glass of milk, Barbara sat down opposite her at the table and sipped her morning coffee.

With breakfast before her, Heather anxiously took off her backpack and set it down on the floor. A few moments later she wiped her plate clean and downed the glass of cold milk. Then, sitting back in her chair, she said, "Martin, my father, is a good man. If it wasn't for the family curse forcing him to play a part in this Innocent Sacrifice, I'm sure he would never have agreed to do it. I realize what it means to the family; no doubt, all of us will be dead soon."

"The Innocent Sacrifice? Explain yourself!" Barbara demanded.

"Yes. That's what we call the virgin daughter, the Innocent Sacrifice. You're involved, too, one way or another. Since you have Bishop genes, there's no escaping it," Heather responded arrogantly.

"I'm trying to understand all of this but not getting anywhere. Explain to me from the beginning. And if you know where my daughter is, then you had better tell me now!"

"No one knows where your daughter is right now other than my father, Brother Tommy, and possibly my stepmother, Eileen. If you go to the police about this, then your daughter will die horribly. You must not try to find out where she is, but I can tell you this much: I overheard my father say your daughter must soon be prepared."

"Prepared for what?" Barbara shouted.

"To die, of course," Heather announced.

"To die?" Barbara repeated and shook her head. She was frustrated with this girl's mysterious speeches and arrogant attitude. "I feel like you are talking in circles. None of what you're saying makes any sense, and if I hadn't seen the things I've seen lately, I'd just call the police and hand you over. Now be straight with me. Cut out the riddles and tell me what's going on!"

"Yes, to die. Your daughter is the sacrifice for the evil monster that controls my father."

"What evil monster are you talking about, Heather?" Barbara asked with growing impatience.

"The Evil my family made a covenant with hundreds of years ago, from what's recorded in our family's archives."

Reaching down into her school backpack, Heather pulled out an ancient-looking leather book and handed it to Barbara. She looked down at the old manuscript; it looked as though it belonged in a museum.

"This is a record of the curse made by an ancestor of mine named Grayson Taylor. My grandmother on the Taylor side told me this is a complete account of what happened to both our families."

Barbara opened the book and began to read aloud, looking up periodically at Heather to confirm the strange tale was real. Each time she did Heather nodded for her to continue.

"Tobias, a young Greek, was a practitioner of the Dark Arts," Barbara read. "A loner, he couldn't stand to be around people; they made him nervous, and he was uncertain of their intentions toward him."

As Barbara continued to read, she forgot about Heather and her warm, modern-day kitchen and began to see an ancient story unfolding before her eyes.

Chapter 19

Tobias wanted more from life than to exist among the peasants and grow old until his death. He began to study under a dark wizard to find a spell to make himself immortal. Although he never learned the secret to immortality, he learned many other evil things.

Tobias lived in a small village near Jamestown, Virginia. One day as he was strolling along the beach and watching the new colonists disembarking from a schooner he noticed a man dressed differently from the other passengers. This gentleman was dressed in black—a pet raven on his shoulder and a large gold medallion around his neck. Few would recognize the mysterious symbol engraved on the medallion unless they practiced magic. Tobias struck up a conversation with the man, and soon a friendship developed between the two.

This sorcerer's name was Shoran McConnell. He came from Scotland, and while they shared a similar interest in magic, there was a difference in how they practiced witchcraft. Shoran, a healer, soon became popular among the villagers.

A few years after Shoran arrived, a new governor was appointed to the colony, and a wave of witch hunts began. Soon suspicion fell on Shoran, and he was captured and tried for practicing witchcraft. His magic did not save him from the flames. Shoran, who had always used his magic to help people, was burned alive for practicing black magic.

Tobias, however, escaped. He had become a wealthy man, and while he still disliked people, he had made himself invaluable by working as the village undertaker. After all, someone needed to bury the corpses that piled up after half the city was accused of witchcraft and murdered.

After Shoran's death Tobias went to his home and found many books of spells and incantations, as well as his pet raven, who he took into his house and cared for as if he was his own pet.

But Tobias also found one more item among Shoran's belongings. It was a dagger, and wrapped around it was a parchment explaining its history and use.

The blade was called the Jillian Dagger. It was infused with powerful magic, its handle was encrusted with jewels, and its metal blade was sharp as a razor. Tobias didn't yet know what to do with it, but he recognized it as ancient and powerful.

As time went on Tobias grew old and bitter toward life in general, realizing that soon the angel of death would be coming for him—a meeting he wanted to avoid at all cost. Also in the village was a man named Augustine Taylor, a chandler by trade. He was married to a woman named Laila, who was of the Bishop bloodline. They had a young daughter named Tessa, who was born crippled. While Augustine had several children, he loved Tessa most. She was gifted with a lovely singing voice.

After working hard at the candlestick shop, Augustine would drag himself home, worn out from all his labor. But when he would hear Tessa sing to welcome him home, all his troubles were forgotten, and his weariness left him.

Unfortunately, Laila was annoyed by all the attention Augustine showered upon Tessa rather than their other children. Laila wanted to rid herself of their disabled daughter. Neither Augustine nor Laila realized someone else in town had turned his attention toward the girl with the lovely voice. The now powerful and rich Tobias hated her ridiculous songs and wanted her singing to end.

As Tessa grew to the age of sixteen, her beautiful voice flourished. Many passersby would stop and listen to her songs. Tobias, too, secretly listened whenever he was near the village, but instead of gaining joy from her beautiful music, the happy songs she sang were painful to his ears.

However, while Tobias seemed to get no pleasure from life, he still craved immortality. Finally, one day, almost by accident, he discovered the secret.

As he mixed ingredients for a spell together in an ancient black cauldron, an explosion occurred, sending shock waves through his bookshelves. They crashed down around him.

Frustrated, he could only curse the mistake he made and clean up the mess.

As he cleaned up the many broken clay jars and glass beakers that had contained the wicked ingredients he used for most of his spells, something in the corner caught his attention: an old parchment of Shoran's that he'd forgotten he had in his possession. Picking it up off the floor, he noticed it was tightly wrapped with three golden chains. He removed the chains, unrolled the scroll, and began to read the ancient text while tugging at his long, gray beard. His pet raven, Hornsby, which had once belonged to Shoran, screeched at him as he deciphered the spell—it was precisely what he had been searching for: an enchantment for achieving immortality by exchanging one's life for another's. It was delightfully intriguing.

According to the parchment, he needed to create a trap to catch an unsuspecting mother and persuade her to give away her child's life for his. Once the bargain was struck, the agreement had to be signed in the mother's blood. The spell must be performed on the night a total lunar eclipse occurred on the winter solstice. As fate would have it, such a rare event was happening within two days. By performing the spell on that day, he would be reborn in the future—the next night a total eclipse fell on the winter solstice—no matter how many hundreds of years in the future that was. Until that day he would exist as a spirit until he was reborn into human form.

As he tried to concentrate on this new spell, he was distracted by the village girl's annoying singing, far off in the distance calling out for her father. In response, shouting out curses, Tobias lost his concentration when suddenly a diabolical plan came to him, and he understood who his victim would be.

He knew little about the candlestick maker or his family except they were poor. Augustine's wife, Laila, would play a role in this cruel game because she was the one who must offer the sacrifice of their daughter. This one act of selfishness that Laila agreed to do would curse her family line—the Bishop family line—for countless generations, including hundreds of years later when, again, one virgin Bishop daughter would have to pay with her life.

Tobias went to see Laila the next day. He knew enough about humankind's love for the precious metal to understand she wouldn't refuse a mountain of gold. He arrived at Taylor's house disguised as a traveling merchant, knocked on the front door, and waited to spring his trap.

When Laila opened the door, she saw a wealthy man dressed in black, with lace cuffs and jeweled buttons. His long, gray hair was tied in a queue and neatly tucked under a feathered hat. He wore white stockings and black shoes with gold buckles and leaned on a shiny black cane topped with a lion's head made of pure gold. In cultured tones he inquired about Tessa, explaining she had the most beautiful voice he'd ever heard.

He told Laila that he wanted to promote her talents in the musical arts, promising she was to have the best things that money could buy. He said his ship was soon sailing and that he had to have an immediate answer or else he couldn't catch the morning tide to exit the harbor.

Laila struggled with what to do, knowing her husband loved Tessa more than anything in the world. But when Tobias ordered his coachmen to bring in six large bags of gold coins and ripped one open, spilling the contents onto the dining table in front of her, she gave away what wasn't hers to give.

Laila couldn't resist, and Tessa, hearing her mother say to the stranger that he could have her, began to cry loudly. She knew she would never again see her father. Her pleas to stay fell on deaf ears as Tobias reached into his pocket and took out a piece of paper, which he handed to Laila.

"There is one little matter we still have to resolve before I leave you," the wizard explained.

"What is that?" Laila inquired.

"You must sign this agreement."

Never taking her eyes from the allure of the gold before her, Laila announced, "You're free to take my daughter. What must I sign?"

Before Laila had a chance to contemplate what she was doing, the wealthy traveler grabbed her hand, pricked her finger, and squeezed the blood that welled up onto the tip of a quill pen.

"Sign this paper, and all this gold will be yours," Tobias said in a menacing voice.

Laila felt afraid but still listened to the stranger's command and gripped the pen, signing her name to the document, thereby condemning her family to a haunting dread for generations to come.

Now Tobias's plans for reincarnation were certain. He wasted no time and ordered his coachmen to carry Taylor's daughter out to the carriage. Without hesitation they picked up Tessa from her bed, took her outside, and drove away, leaving an astonished Laila behind with her newfound piles of gold.

Later that afternoon Augustine closed his shop and came home. But he knew something was dreadfully wrong as he turned down their street. He didn't hear his daughter's voice. He ran to his house and threw open the door. Inside his wife sat next to a pile of gold, looking dazed.

"Where is Tessa?"

"Tessa has been offered a new life elsewhere by a wealthy benefactor so her gifts will be recognized for all the world to see. Now look, Augustine, at all the gold the stranger gave us."

"What are you saying?" Looking lost, Augustine broke down and cried out, "Tell me, who could be a better benefactor than her father? What have you done, Laila? What have you done to our daughter?"

Hearing her husband's cries, Laila realized too late that she had sold something priceless belonging to her husband— no amount of gold would make up for the loss of his daughter. She also realized too late what her blind jealousy had made her do.

"Go! Take your gold, and get out!" Augustine commanded.

Panic seized her as she realized what a costly mistake she had just made. She couldn't carry all of the gold with her so she grabbed the remains of one bag and ran out of the house and down the street, looking for someone who would help her carry the gold.

What she didn't realize was the entire town enjoyed

hearing Tessa's singing, and they had witnessed what she had done and saw her daughter being taken away in the carriage. Everyone she asked to help her turned their backs to her. Realizing everyone in the village would scorn her, she decided to get Tessa back. She went to the docks, looking for the ship that she prayed hadn't sailed.

Running desperately through the narrow streets, Laila came upon two drunken men. Recognizing them as the ones who had carried Tessa from her house earlier that day, she approached them and begged for their help. Confronted by the distraught mother, the men began to laugh wildly and told her the man wasn't a wealthy merchant but the old undertaker who lived near the cemetery on the edge of town.

"Why, then, would he want Tessa?" she cried.

"We don't have any idea." The man's words were slurred and barely audible. "But the gentleman paid us handsomely for little or no work."

Laila ran as fast as she could toward Tobias's house. Finally, she reached the cemetery. It was approaching dusk, and she became frightened by the prospect of dead bodies in their graves. It was then when she realized she had cursed their beautiful daughter to the same fate.

Pushing her fear aside, Laila continued along the road until in the distance she saw the light coming from a window in the stone house. Pounding madly on the old wooden door, she got no response. She began crying, wanting desperately to get inside to save her daughter before it was too late. To her surprise the door creaked open, and standing before her was the evil wizard, dressed in a black silk embroidered overcoat and wearing a pointed hat.

Laila shouted angrily at him to give Tessa back and threw down the bag of gold at his feet.

"What do you want from me? There is nothing here that belongs to you," he replied to her sharply.

Laila pleaded again for him to give Tessa back to her.

Tobias laughed. "Go away from here, you foolish woman. Go home, and count your gold. You no longer have a daughter; she belongs to me!"

"Where is Tessa?" she begged again.

"Soon to be sacrificed," he laughed. "You cannot help Tessa now. Go away and leave me in peace."

"No! I must see my daughter!" Laila shouted desperately and pushed through the door. Staggering through the foyer, she cried out Tessa's name throughout the house, her voice echoing in the hollowness of his dark abode. After searching every room on the first floor, she returned to Tobias and demanded to know where he kept her.

The angry sorcerer turned around and said, "Get out before you die, too, you foolish woman!"

"I do not care," Laila responded. "Where is she?"

She again called Tessa's name. She desperately ran up the stairs to the second story, searching for her daughter, only to find dark and musty rooms with tattered curtains and several dead animals, including bears and mountain lions preserved in frightening poses. Her daughter was nowhere in sight.

Suddenly, she heard Tessa call her from a room at the end of the hall; she ran to it and entered a much larger room with a high ceiling, at least twenty feet above the floor. In the corner was a large fireplace, glowing red. Tessa was strapped to a large stone table. She ran to her daughter and tried to free her from her imprisonment. She didn't notice the sharp, jewel-encrusted dagger twirling above Tessa's body, ready to fall and administer death at any second. Next to the table, lit by a tall candle, an ancient scroll lay open, ready to be read.

"Mother, why did you sell me to that monster?" Tessa cried. "Why would you do that? Don't you know I love you?"

Before Laila could answer she let out a deep groan and collapsed to the floor with a blade sticking out of her back. Standing behind her was the evil sorcerer, who laughed loudly and answered, "It doesn't matter any longer whether she believes your love is real. What matters is the fact that she sold you to me. Your mother's sacrifice will bring me immortality."

Pulling the dagger free from Laila, he added, 'It's almost time for you to die. We are only waiting for one more participant in our little game, child. It's your father."

Tessa listened in horror as the evil man, proud of his accomplishment, explained how this spell was to play out.

"Child, you see, the twirling dagger above your heart? It's infused with a unique incantation-activated trigger. Soon your father will arrive, searching for his lovely daughter. Your father named Taylor, seeing you in danger, will merely have to touch the handle of the blade. At that moment it will magically stop twirling and lock into your father's palm. Then it will slowly move downward until it ultimately plunges through your beating heart.

"What, you may ask, if you warn your father of the appending doom? Sadly, you will be unable to say anything at all!" The wizard laughed as he strolled over to a broken shelf and took down a small glass vile. "This potion will prevent you from speaking or warning your father of the trap I've set."

Before he could administer it to her, Tessa said, "I forgive you. I cannot say why your heart is so hateful toward me, but you should know that in my heart I've forgiven you."

"Child, regardless of your feelings toward me, I have no ill will toward you; you are simply a means to an end. You see, I cannot achieve immortality without spilling your blood." Tobias smiled and poured a few drops of liquid down her throat.

Time passed quickly, and it grew dark. As the full moon rose in the night sky, it began to darken as the sun passed in front of it, on its way to a total lunar eclipse. Reaching for a scroll near the table, Tobias explained that he would soon be traveling on a journey of both time and space. Now that he had the agreement signed in Laila's blood, he was forever leaving behind his weak mortal body and the world he hated.

"As I take your life from you, I will transpose into darkness without form or body and will exist as a spirit, only to reappear at the next lunar eclipse, five hundred years into the future. A male of the Taylor name—your name, Tessa—will have a mark on his hand that will appear, signifying he is the one chosen to take the life of a virgin Bishop daughter. The Taylor male must use the Jillian Dagger to perform the act or else he will sacrifice in vain. Only the dagger and the spell will be successful."

His plan was complete; Tobias turned to the black raven and called him over. Squawking loudly, it landed on his shoulder.

Turning back to the helpless girl, he announced with pleasure, "I want you both to understand that soon my raven, Hornsby, will dine on your lovely eyes, along with the rest of you,"

Turning to the bird, he coyly asked, "Won't you eat well, my pet?"

The large black bird squawked as if it somehow knew what he meant.

Unknown to the powerful wizard, Laila was still alive, hanging on desperately to any fleeting hope of rescue. She heard everything the old sorcerer said but sadly, could only lie there dying, unable to move as her life passed away.

The town's clock tower rung twelve times, announcing midnight. The lunar eclipse was total. The wizard began to read aloud from the ancient scroll in a language Tessa had never heard before. When he had finished, a sheer curtain fell around him, making him and his pet invisible to anyone in the room. As if on cue, the distant sound of horse hooves were approaching the house. The front door swung open below, and Augustine called out Tessa's name.

Tessa tried desperately to warn her father, but she couldn't speak. When Augustine entered the room, he saw his daughter chained to a cold stone table. Ignoring her grunts and groans, he grabbed hold of the dagger to move it away from her. Instead, his hand acted on its own, and his fingers wrapped themselves around the handle of the blade. Unable to let go, though he tried with all his strength, the knife descended into his daughter's body.

In horror he could only watch as the blade's point slowly penetrated her chest. Her blood began to pour out as her heart was cut asunder; it struggled to beat the life-giving blood within her body.

Seeing the pain on his precious daughter's face, Augustine cried out her name and collapsed on the floor. As if by magic, his hand was set free. Subsequently, he saw a dark scar marring his flesh.

To Augustine's horror, Tobias, the wizard, suddenly appeared in the room, a raven on his shoulder. He was almost transparent, a plume of smoke streaming upward. He vanished into a thunderous red cloud of vapor.

Seeing his master change into nothingness, Hornsby the raven also flew within the reddish cloud and vanished. Lying on the stone table, the tears of the innocent ran down Tessa's cheeks as she died. Now free to speak, with dying lips, Tessa whispered, "I forgive you, Mother, for what you have done."

Laila, dying, knew she must explain the curse to her husband. Spitting out blood as she spoke, Laila described the curse in detail, saying a member of the Taylor family must sacrifice a virgin girl from the Bishop family. This ritual must be performed on the next lunar eclipse five hundred years into the future—this coinciding with the winter solstice. As a word of warning, she said, if a Taylor ancestor refuses, the powerful sorcerer Tobias will come to life and murder every one of the Taylor ancestries horribly.

When her last bit of strength, Laila stood to her feet and looked upon her dying daughter. Breaking out in tears, she cried out, "I love you, Tessa," then collapsed to the floor, dead.

Augustine remained at the old house until the following day. When the morning light shone through the window, it reflected off the precious stones inlaid on the hilt of the dagger and glittered brightly. Seeing his daughter dead with the Jillian Dagger still thrust in her chest, Augustine walked over, ripped it free, and decided to hide it somewhere no one would ever be able to find it.

But he was wrong.

After loosening the bonds that held his daughter captive, he lifted her from the sacrificial table and carried her home. As he entered the town, a small group of townsfolk saw him bringing Tessa in his arms. The news soon spread, and all the villagers came out to see the sight of the lonely man carrying his daughter.

His other children came out of their house when he reached home and followed Augustine to the family cemetery. Tessa, the one pleasure in his life, was gone, and he dug a single grave in the Taylor family plot and buried her there.

Not one of the Taylor family members ever sang or played joyful music again. His eldest son, Grayson, recorded the tragic event for prosperity and began a journal describing everything his father told him in detail. The day came when Augustine died, leaving only one request: to be buried next to Tessa, where they rest even to this day.

According to the legend, when Augustine returned to the old house to retrieve his wife's body, he found a small crystal object in a crevice on the stone altar where his daughter's body had lain. He picked it up and placed it in his pocket. Augustine hoisted Laila's body over his shoulder and carried it out of the house. Upon leaving, he grabbed hold of a burning torch and threw it against the shabby curtains, setting the house ablaze.

That night he chose to bury his wife's remains in the Bishop family plot. Inside, along with her body, he placed the Jillian Dagger and a manuscript titled "The Book of Magical Spells." He included all the gold that was used to purchase his daughter. He covered the grave with dirt, refusing to set a headstone or marker in an attempt to be forgotten.

Chapter 20

Barbara slowly closed the hard leather cover and asked, "Why has my family never heard of any of this before? All of this concerns my family and me. Now we are the helpless victims of one senseless act performed by a desperate woman centuries ago."

"The Bishop family was never to know their bloodline would one day provide a sacrifice," said Heather. "How was it possible to tell your children the truth that you were born with this curse to be sacrificed?"

Glancing up at the clock on the wall, Barbara realized she was running late to pick up Rachel from school. Although it was just past noon, she remembered she got out early because of a parent-teacher conference that day.

"All this talk about death makes me feel insecure about leaving my daughter on a curb, waiting for me to show up," she said. "Can we finish this at another time? It all sounds like a fairy tale to me, but I need to know more."

She grabbed her purse and started to leave as Heather blurted out, "I haven't told you how my family discovered the Jillian Dagger. No one believed it to be tangible until strange things started happening to my family and we began seeing the phantom Tobias for ourselves. Don't you see? It's all true, and now it's affecting you as well."

"Meet me tomorrow, please," Barbara suggested. "And then you can finish telling me about your family."

Heather paused. "I don't know if I can."

"Why not?"

"I can't go back to my parents' house. My family will try to prevent me from coming to see you."

"But why would they try to do that?"

Staring into Barbara's eyes, Heather asked, "Did you notice the blue station wagon that has circled your block at least three times since I've been here talking to you?"

"What blue station wagon?" Barbara asked, taken by surprise by the question.

"Never mind," Heather said. "If they catch me, I won't be allowed to live."

"What? Here you go again with the mysteries, Heather. What exactly are you saying now?" Barbara asked, in a hurry to pick up her daughter.

"Never mind, Mrs. Harding. It's all right. I'll try to return if I can. It would be best if you remembered to keep the crystal close; it has immeasurable power you can't imagine. Whoever gave it to you must know of its power. Be safe, and take care of yourself!" Heather shouted and headed toward the back door.

Barbara yelled after her, "What about your family journal? Don't you want it back?"

"You can keep it," Heather replied. "I have a feeling it won't help anyone now, especially since Tobias is coming back to life." She unlocked the door, ran into the backyard, and disappeared over the fence.

Alone, Barbara sought to absorb all the family history, especially the curse. It was a curse; after all, there's no other way to explain the facts. No, knowing the truth didn't ease the pain of Melissa's disappearance and that she was kidnapped, destined for murder. It was a truth Barbara refused to accept.

She stared down at the tattered and torn book, no doubt from the years of abuse by the Taylor family, as the lessons were taught that one day a family member would be called forth to commit murder. She'd forgotten she needed to go pick up Rachel; she'd forgotten everything except the need to fight this evil.

Suddenly, behind her a conspicuous, evil darkness arrived in the kitchen. Barbara sensed it immediately as the air in the room had become frigid. She shivered and turned slowly, knowing what she would see. There in front of her, in full view, was the shadowy poltergeist of Tobias. Was he more solid than when she had seen him before? Or was it just that she knew what to expect now: an older man, bearded, and wearing the clothes of centuries past, an evil leer on his face. Tobias's form swirled in a dark mist, from the floor up to the kitchen ceiling. It blocked the door. There was no way she could get past it.

"Now, my dear, you know my story—tell me, what do you intend to do?"

The shape's mouth didn't move. She heard his voice only in her head. Was this a nightmare? Was she hallucinating?

No. Barbara still held the old book in her hands. It was solid and real. Staring intently back at the monster, unafraid, she shouted, "You monster—I will not allow you to murder my daughter. I will fight you with all I have to give!"

"Hmmm, unlike the other weak mortal who quickly sold her daughter into bondage, you seem to be willing to fight for your child."

"With all my soul I will fight you until you are defeated, you devil. Know this: You cannot win, no matter what, because I will never agree to it! I understand you need me to sell Melissa away. You need me to sign our agreement in blood.

Now that I know who you are and what you're up to, you can never win."

"Sad, pathetic human with all your frailties. You will lose this fight." The voice whispered in her head. It was evil, malevolent; it filled her with despair, even as she shook her head, denying what it said.

"It's best to concede and give up now. Use the time you have left to enjoy your last days on the earth; after all, your time is short. Forget about your daughter; you can never save her. Her days are counted for slaughter, you fool!"

Barbara was shaking. She wanted to hide, to run away, but somehow she found her courage. She stood tall and straight and looked directly into the face of the demon shadow.

"Oh, it's sad that even after five hundred years you don't understand the heart of a mother. What you see as weakness is a hidden force of love and devotion toward my child that will eventually destroy you."

"No, you're wrong; I will show you an example of your frailty."

Tobias quickly, without warning, gripped Barbara around the neck. She began to cough; her face turned red as she gasped for air. The reality was the demon was a spirit and still possessed enough power to cross over into the physical world to move any object by his will or assert his resolve on the mortal flesh, Barbara wondered, even as she knew she was dying.

No! she thought to herself. *This cannot be the end. If I die now, who will save Melissa?*

She gasped in vain, trying to find the slightest breath of air, anything to help her live one more minute, one more second. Then she remembered the crystal. It was in her pocket. She somehow found the strength to move her hand—slowly, ever so slowly—toward her pants pocket. There she felt the small hard object and withdrew it. Gasping, she reached out and jabbed it at the ghostly eyes of the shadowy demon. Tobias winced in pain and let go of his grip around Barbara's throat.

Coughing and gasping, Barbara leaned against the kitchen counter and struggled to catch her breath. Out of the corner of her eye she glimpsed Tobias's ghostly image disappearing from view. The shadow no longer obscured the door to the hallway. The crystal's brilliant light illuminated the room with its beautiful blue light.

Shouting at the demon, Barbara cried, "You will not win this fight. I will die before giving up!"

There was no response from the shadows. Nothing. Who would believe Barbara's story? Who would help her? Certainly not her husband. If she told Mark about this latest experience, he would have her locked up in a psychiatric ward immediately.

The police? Certainly not Lieutenant Reed. He'd politely shake his head, tell everyone she had cracked under the strain of losing her daughter, and help Mark drive her to the psychiatric ward. There was Susan. She was fascinated with Barbara's stories, but it was all a game to her. She didn't really believe it. Sterling had given her the crystal, and he had given her advice; he had accepted her story. But could she count on him for anything more?

The demon was gone; it was as if he never existed except for the memory of its boney fingers around her throat, choking her to death. *Death*, Barbara thought, *was it the final price I should pay to save my daughter?*

**Read on for a sneak peek
of**

The

Family

Curse

Book Two of
The Bishops' Sacrifice

Martin woke up thinking it was just another average Saturday morning, nothing extraordinary. After breakfast he planned to cut the lawn, as usual, and when he finished the yard work he wanted to relax in his hammock, have a cold beer, and fall asleep smelling the freshly cut grass clippings. But when Martin got up that morning, there on his right hand he noticed a bright red spot, which made him think perhaps something had bitten him.

He felt sick to his stomach. He hated spiders and killed them every chance he got. If a spider had bitten him, hopefully, it wasn't a brown recluse; if that was the case, he'd better see a doctor to be examined.

As he looked closely at the mark, it didn't look or feel like a spider bite. It looked more like a rash. Without warning he felt light-headed and dizzy and held onto the bathroom counter to stabilize himself from falling. Then, taking him by surprise, he heard a commanding voice in his head saying: *Taylor, you have been chosen to fulfill your destiny to sacrifice the innocent.*

He shook his head to regain his senses but nothing seemed to work, and he felt his body and mind being taken over by the intrusion of the dark force.

Taylor, I command you to obey.

He felt his will and control start to wane. As he looked at his reflection in the mirror, he saw a blackness that appeared inside the bathroom. It completely enveloped him, and he couldn't resist its power.

He was no longer himself and surrendered to whatever evil existence had captured him. Soon his words and thoughts were no longer his own. There in the mirror, instead of his reflection, he saw something evil looking back at him, something that moved within his consciousness. He knew all was lost. Words flowed from him that he couldn't have believed possible, and without any resistance he said, "What is your command, Master?"

Once he surrendered his consciousness, he began to see things he couldn't have believed possible: what was once invisible such as time and other dimensions. And he also saw humanity through the eyes of his new guest. He began to understand the frailty of man, who was a weak, pathetic, selfish creature. Being empowered by the darkness gave him a new understanding, and the world in which he lived became nothing to him.

Only now did he know what the creature was, and he accepted his guest with a willing admission of defeat. While this evil one named Tobias haunted his thoughts, he received a history lesson from the ancient source, who was prone to curse man as he talked freely about what he planned to do once set free in his new body.

After Martin surrendered to his new master, something unexpected happened: The dark creature was no longer just a faceless voice in the darkness. Martin started to see the figure of a wretched old man. From behind the curtain that separated the two worlds, he was barely able to see the shape of his master as he spoke, who now inhabited his existence.

The next day after his encounter with his new dark master, the urgency of what he must do took priority over his life. Without telling his family where he was going, he left the house for Massachusetts the following morning to retrieve the Jillian Dagger. Tobias had explained where it got its name; it was called the Jillian Dagger after an ancient Norman queen named Jillian, who used it to kill her husband, the king, taking revenge for what he had done to her lover and family. It was a sad, dark tale of betrayal and heartbreak.

Yes, the story, he thought. It was similar to his life and equally tragic. *One can never tell what part fate will play in your life. How different and yet the same are our tales of tragedy. I'm being forced to use the dagger to kill an innocent virgin, yet the blade was already used by someone who thought she was justified to kill her husband, the king.*

Driving the interstate, he wondered how on earth he was going to find an unmarked grave of someone who'd died so long ago. His fears and worries dissolved by the knowledge that Tobias had told him earlier that he would reveal the grave's location and take care of it all.

Confident he was heading in the right direction, he sat back and got comfortable for the long drive. With time on his hands, his mind drifted to the story behind the dagger. *According to Tobias's report, an English king named Osborn had a beautiful young wife he loved. However, just as kings and other mighty men were easily controlled by their emotions and could give away their hearts to attractive young admirers, so could a queen. The difference was that when a king's heart was emotionally ripped out, usually his subjects paid the price for the betrayal.*

When Martin finally arrived in Massachusetts, using the magical powers connected to Tobias, he knew the dagger was buried in one of the Bishop family plots and would soon find it. As he drew closer to his prize, a new desire burned within him that he never felt before, and it drove him crazy.

Still, his frail human body was limited and could only do so much. Feeling exhausted from the drive and search, he decided it was best to check into a hotel close to the old cemetery, where he felt the most potent energy of the dagger's power.

That night was to be moonless, which would fit perfectly with his plans. Sometime after midnight he left the hotel and walked down the street toward the old cemetery. He carried a shovel and a flashlight to light his way. The streets were deserted and silent; nothing moved around him. In some locations eerie shadows lay hidden by the buildings.

When he arrived at the old cemetery, all was peaceful

and quiet—no one anywhere at that time of night. Of course, if the authorities caught him, he would have a hard time explaining why he'd dug up an ancient grave, but something burned within him that was overpowering. Martin couldn't have resisted even if he'd wanted to. He felt he had to retrieve the dagger at all costs—not only the blade but a book of magic as well. Hopefully, he could save his family with the powers hidden within this book of magic by helping this poltergeist.

About the Author

I was raised on the sunny beaches of Southern California. As a young boy, I spent many summers swimming and playing in the ocean without care. Later as the man, I was fortunate enough to land a job in Aerospace, working for McDonnell Douglas. There I worked on military aircraft and, most exciting of all, rockets! All types of space hardware, including the space station, space shuttle, and the Delta rocket.

My life has always been interesting—a father to four children and two stepchildren, a grandfather to fourteen. I've given away my heart to all. In my life I've always loved writing. My first experience at being creative was describing my feelings through poetry, which I did with mixed emotions. But it wasn't until I put pencil to the paper that my imagination soared, and I was set free to explore all the possibilities of creating an exciting story.

Here and now is the result of my work.

Acknowledgments

My mother, Maxine, who believed in my abilities as a storyteller and was the very first reader of my work.

My sister, Peggie, who enthusiastically purchased my first published book.

My cousin Harvey, whose words of encouragement meant everything.

Friends Hal and Mark, who are both eager to push me to success.